MAKING SENSE OF ME

FAYE COX

MAKING SENSE OF ME
ISBN: 978-1-7391831-0-3

First published in Great Britain
in 2022 through Amazon
self-publishing service

Disclaimer: Real names/places
have been changed to protect the identities.
Permission has been granted to use case studies.
Always seek the advice of your doctor or other qualified
health provider regarding a medical condition.

Designed and Produced by
Miss Digital Media

DEDICATIONS

This is a book for my younger self and a guide for any young girl trying to make sense of her world.

CONTENTS

ACKNOWLEDGEMENTS

Thanks to my daughters Ruby and Darcy, who inspire me each and every day.

AUTHOR BIO

Faye Cox is a professional Life Coach and NLP Practitioner working with teenagers and their families, creating a deeper connection through better communication with themselves and each other. Faye also works with schools and colleges to bring young people's well-being and emotional intelligence to the forefront of education.

She has been featured in The Metro, The Guardian, The Telegraph and Stylist Magazine, and local radio.

Faye deeply believes that **Well-being leads to Well-doing.**

FOREWORD

It was such an honour to be asked to write the Foreword for Faye Cox's long-awaited and well-needed book for teens: Making Sense of Me. I first began to communicate online with Faye several years ago. She has always demonstrated a deep passion for supporting and empowering young people. She has become a member of an awesome and inspiring tribe of people who understand the importance of empowering younger generations to know their worth and stand in their own power of self-belief.

The chapters capture Faye's wealth of knowledge and experience as a coach for vulnerable young people and illustrate her ability to fine-tune carefully thought-out solutions to meet the needs of young people. I love that the chapters are filled with real-life examples.

The book is very insightful and captures pertinent topics for young people today, with chapters on relationships, social media, self-harm, self-compassion, anxiety and stress. As a Psychologist, I am fully aware of the mental health challenges young people face and how debilitating it can be if they cannot think of solutions to the feelings and emotions they are experiencing. Books like this are so important for reinforcing the importance of self-care, self-development and self-empowerment.

This is a book that parents, teachers and young people

will be encouraged to work with and learn a lot from. This book allows those important icky tricky conversations to be started and continued with confidence... Enjoy the read and have a pencil at hand to take notes and action.

Dr Michele McDowell
Educational and Child Psychologist

CHAPTER ONE

CLEARING THE FOG

You're instantly referred to as 'a bundle of joy' when you're born. Everyone smiled and made weird noises at you. They looked at you with so much love in their eyes, and to them, you were magical.

When you did a burp, it was celebrated and messing in your nappy was a proud moment. But then, as you got older, your parents and the world told you to hide your burps and not talk about your 'movements' in public, so it's not surprising that over the years, you've picked up some very confusing messages about yourself!

As you enter your teenage years, things get even more confusing. You step beyond your family unit and explore other people's values, opinions and ideas about the world. Your friends become a significant influence as you need greater independence and autonomy over your life. Your parents start to become uncool in your eyes, and you begin to see them a little differently. They almost appear older overnight, and hanging out with them is a big no-no unless you want a lift somewhere, and even then, you want them to drop you up the road from where you're meeting your friends.

You feel your parents understand you less and that you don't know them as well anymore. You might start to relate to your friend's parents more than your own, and your siblings may seem like complete strangers or the most annoying

creatures that ever roamed this planet! Their mere existence in your room is enough for you to pick a fight with them, so they'll leave you alone. The age gap between you and them feels far greater than ever before, even if it's only a couple of years in reality.

As you take in even more people's opinions of you, this can create even more confusion. You can start to believe things to be true for you when in fact, they're not. For example, if an older sibling has ever told you that they're better than you at running, yet you've never raced them, which has been something they have repeatedly said. Their friend has agreed with them, and you may take this personally and begin to think this is true. You may hold on to this so-called truth for many years when it's just two people's opinions on it. The opinions are likely based on their reality and perfection - not on fact or who you really are on the inside.

Throughout this book, I want you to remember that you're still that bundle of joy and always will be. You are loved, and you are worthy. In this book, we'll rediscover that joy by creating more self-acceptance. We're going to clear the fog and let go of some of those mixed messages about yourself so you can be more confident, more accepting and more yourself.

Consider this book your lifelong toolkit and guide you can pass on to friends and family and even your daughter one day!

CHAPTER TWO

WHO ARE YOU?

Have you ever felt a little lost and confused with who you are and where you fit in?

Is this causing you some level of stress and anxiety?

Are you looking for something that feels just a little bit out of reach on an average day? Something that you can't quite grasp, but you know deep down that it's there. You see others around you who appear to have it; some seem to have it in bucket loads and ooze it, while others have what you consider to be just enough, but all look like they have something you don't.

As a girl who was more introverted and believed that to BE good enough, I needed to BE louder, BE brighter and BE more popular, I know how this feels. I spent years trying to be somebody I wasn't, to fit in, be accepted, and feel good enough. I went out of my way to create this person who wasn't me. A person who looked on the outside like she was more confident, more accepting and more extroverted when my confidence and self-esteem were low underneath it. I felt like I was a fake, and my stress and anxiety levels rose as I drifted further and further away from who I really was.

I believed that to BE good enough; I had to BE the perfect child, the perfect student. Look perfect, sound perfect, BE perfect. In actual fact, I needed to get to know and accept myself for the deep thinker, empathetic, kind and generous

girl that I really was and embrace everything that comes with such a powerful personality. I needed to BE more ME and less everyone else!

You may be feeling something similar. You may feel like all your friends are more popular, more out there, more confident or more academic. Perhaps you feel like you're not being seen or heard by friends and family when you try to talk about how you're feeling. Instead, you may take yourself off to your room rather than face any conversation about what's going on for you. You feel like no one understands, like no one is paying attention and that you're not fully in control of what's happening to and around you.

Despite all this, you've learned to be too hard on yourself when things go wrong. You're not showing yourself enough compassion due to the confusion over how you should behave, show up, and BE.

What would showing up for yourself look like? How would it feel to be able to show up as yourself fully? A more confident and accepting version of yourself?

How do you want to feel when you look in the mirror and see the real, authentic, amazing you? Who recognises and focuses on her strengths, individuality, and powerful personality. The one who fully accepts themselves and knows she deserves all the happiness in the world.

How would it feel to know that YOU ARE ENOUGH NO MATTER WHAT?

CHAPTER THREE

WHY LISTEN TO ME?

From a very early age, I didn't feel good enough. As the youngest sibling, I never felt like I had much autonomy over what happened in my life. I never felt seen or heard as there was always so much going on in the lives of those around me. I threw myself into reading to escape the world around me. I was a shy child who never strayed far from my mum's side. I would stand outside of what was happening and observe everything before joining in. I did this at every party I went to. I was the child who didn't join in until it was nearly time to go home and didn't want to leave.

I experienced bullying from about ten years old, first from my gymnastics coach and then from other kids at school. Having had little control over my life at home, I became what my peers called 'bossy'. This is something I see a lot in the younger siblings that I now work with. Having little control at home spilt over into my life at school, and I used this space to try and gain the control I needed. When I look back now, I can see this clearly; it was something I wish I had known back then. Autonomy is one of our emotional needs, becoming more important as we reach those teenage years.

At school, I was pretty clever. I was in the top sets for most things. Maths was my weakest subject, and to be honest, it still is, but I have mastered what I need for everyday life and overcome the mindset that I was no good at it. I was a conscientious student until I reached year 10, when

everything seemed to unravel. At the time, I had no idea why. Still, having gone back to my teenage years to unpick the old beliefs and heal from some of my experiences, I concluded that this happened because I got lost.

After being bullied for so many years for being too short, my ears slightly sticking out, being too quiet, too conscientious, too posh, too introverted (the list goes on!) - I had unconsciously changed my whole self to FIT IN. I had become so far removed from the real me that I was living in a place of stress and anxiety from being someone I wasn't. Someone I hardly recognised. Yet, at the time, it had worked. My peers were more accepting of me being louder and not so clever. I felt bigger just by being louder. Yet I had clearly become unhappier within myself. I began to act out, became quite gobby and rude, and now when I think about it, it was all to cover the fact that I was unhappy with who I had become. My actions were not in line with my values as a person.

Through this time, my confidence grew, or at least I thought it was confidence. However, my self-esteem was low underneath it all. Although I felt good enough for others, I didn't feel good about myself. It went on for years, and I used various methods to hide and cover up the shame I felt about myself. I became very critical of people, particularly of other girls. I now know that this was me projecting the parts of myself I wasn't happy with onto these girls. At the time, though, I thought it was what you did, tearing other girls down to make yourself feel better - but it didn't work. I didn't feel any better about myself at all. All it did was further embed my beliefs that I wasn't good enough. I had, in fact, turned into the girls I had been hiding from all those years - the ones who took their insecurities out on me.

As a mum of two beautiful and amazingly unique girls, I have learned much from them. I also work with young people as a qualified Coach and Practitioner using a variation of NLP, CBT and Mindfulness to support them in building confidence and increasing self-esteem and resilience whilst reducing stress and anxiety.

I want this to be your valuable handbook to help you build solid emotional intelligence, a lifetime resource I wish I'd had in my teenage years and one my two girls have also received. I contemplated taking my own life when I was 19 after my split with my first serious boyfriend and not having the tools I needed. If I had been able to quieten the negative voices in my mind from an earlier age, it would have made my late teens and early 20's an entirely different experience.

Since working with young girls struggling with their self-worth, who are experiencing stress and anxiety due to feeling lost and not good enough, special enough, deserving enough, confident enough, pretty enough, clever enough, or popular enough, I want to ensure that every young girl who reads this book knows that they ARE GOOD ENOUGH - NO MATTER WHAT!

CHAPTER FOUR

What Else Can You Do?

As a young girl, it can feel both frightening and frustrating when everything starts to change physically, emotionally and within the environment around you.

It's a time when you can begin to feel isolated like you no longer belong in certain groups of people at school and your social circles. You can start feeling a little lost and invisible to those around you and wonder how to navigate these changes.

Around this time, you may develop negative thought patterns around who you are and where you fit. Doubting yourself, your friendships, and your place within your family dynamic may become your new norm. As a result, you become disconnected from friends you were once so close to, to family members who used to be the people you would always turn to when things went wrong.

Your behaviours may change and become riskier as you struggle to understand yourself. Friends and family may find it challenging to understand and deal with, especially as you also find it difficult to explain.

Parents and caregivers will likely have given you advice, but you're still getting the same results. Teachers may have spoken to you about your change in behaviour or their concerns that you may be withdrawing and losing focus on your learning. However, you still feel the same way.

To try and make yourself and those around you feel better, you may take on the role of a people pleaser. Changing things about yourself to fit back in, even though those changes and behaviours go against what you truly believe in - is that making you happy?

You begin to drift further and further away from your real self, causing your confidence and self-esteem to lower. Meanwhile, you become more influenced by those you mistakenly believe have everything sorted in life - people you now see as more confident than you. It works in the short term. But as time goes on, this affects your self-esteem and confidence even more as you begin to believe that these people are better than you and that you are not good enough as you are.

As a teenager, I did the same thing and changed my whole self to 'fit in.' I repeated a specific pattern of behaviour. I became angry and withdrawn. As a result, I lost myself, my confidence and some of my real friends. It made me feel worse about myself after a while, as I was disconnecting with myself and those closest to me to fit in with people who, when I look back, weren't my people.

CHAPTER FIVE

ON THE OTHER SIDE

On the other side of low self-esteem, lack of confidence, frustration and isolation is self-acceptance. A feeling like no other. A feeling that YOU ARE GOOD ENOUGH NO MATTER WHAT.

It's a place where your confidence grows, your self-esteem increases, and you learn to create healthy boundaries for yourself and others. You realise that your stress and anxiety symptoms have reduced. By discovering how to re-balance your physical and emotional needs providing you with more clarity, calm and compassion, you can then pass it on to the people around you.

Self-acceptance is where you no longer need approval from others; you approve of yourself from the inside out.

You build a stronger relationship with yourself that no one can take away from you, and you learn to show up as your authentic, fabulous and real self. This alone will attract other genuine people into your life.

When you show yourself more love, kindness and compassion, it allows you the space to understand what you need at any given moment. It enables you to PAUSE and go back to your values and work out if your actions are aligned with those values and how to resolve the conflict you may be feeling inside.

Starting your journey to self-acceptance will set you on the path to a happy, healthy, and successful life.

I worked with a young girl who I could see was trying her best to fit in with the girls in her friendship group. As time went by, I witnessed her change her whole self to be like them. She started dressing like them, doing the same things as them and treating people the way they did. But as more time passed, I saw this young girl change into someone she wasn't, and I could see that with every week that went by, she was disconnecting from her authentic self. She became angrier, and her behaviour became erratic until she reached the point where she withdrew almost completely. She became mentally exhausted as she lived a life that wasn't hers. That wasn't who she was. She was out of alignment with her values, causing her a lot of stress.

When she finally realised what was happening, she bravely decided to go back out there and be herself. It took some encouragement and support, but eventually, I witnessed her return to her real self with a smile back on her face. Having started the journey to self-acceptance, she could see that those worth having in her life would accept her for who she was, not what she was.

CHAPTER SIX

VALUES, BELIEFS AND BOUNDARIES

It is safe for me to change and grow.

What do we mean when we talk about values and beliefs?

As human beings, we all have our very own map of the world. No two people's are ever the same. You can be an identical twin, yet your world map will still differ.

No other person has experienced life through your lens. No other person has seen, heard or felt things exactly the same way you have. This is hugely beneficial to learn as it can relieve the pressure of feeling like you have to be like other people.

VALUES

Values are the things that are important to you. I call these your non-negotiables in life. For example, my values are honesty, compassion, empathy and respect. I live by these values, and when I feel one of them is not being met either by myself or by those closest to me, it can cause stress and anxiety. I'll discuss stress, anxiety and needs in the relevant chapter.

Beliefs are what you believe to be true about yourself and the world around you. These can be anything from thinking that you're not good enough at something, not tall enough

for something or even that you can't do something for whatever reason you've convinced yourself is true.

When you're a young child, your values and beliefs are automatically the same as those closest to you: your parents, older siblings, grandparents, etc. But when you reach your teenage years, your actual values can get lost and confused with other people's. You can even begin to doubt your family values and believe other families' values align with what you want to believe. These beliefs may suit your current lifestyle more, or they might be more relaxed, and that's okay. It's completely normal to question what you believe to be true and what your parents believe to be true as long as you do it respectfully. Remember, your parents may have lived by these values for a long time and will be deeply embedded in their minds. For someone to come along and question them can feel difficult and uncomfortable and like someone is disrespecting them. As with most parents, they may not even know why they have them in the first place, as they too will have inherited some of their beliefs from their parents a long time ago.

When I was a child, my parents firmly believed that drawing on anything apart from paper was wrong. I know this was to stop me from writing on the walls when I was a toddler. Your parents may have told you the same thing. As an adult, I can realise what this means. Still, as a young child, this became so embedded in my mind that I believed that I was never to draw on anything except paper. When my children suggested that we draw a rainbow on the pavement for the NHS during COVID, my instant reply was 'no.' To which they both asked me why. I gave them the old 'because I said so' answer and thought that would be the end of it. But then they asked me why it was so wrong and gave me two very valid reasons why it should be okay; one being that it was to show support for the NHS and the other that they could easily wash it off. Well, what could I say? I had nothing; no comeback could back up this belief my parents had given me as a young child. I even asked myself why and to my amazement, I had no real reason. I had acted instantly and unconsciously due to something drummed into me as a child. I'm sure you can guess what happened next - I told them we could get some chalk and create our rainbow. Their faces were a picture, and our rainbow was the talk of the close and stayed put until the rain came and washed it all away a few days later.

Why am I telling you about my old belief and rainbows? I want you to know that even we adults have old and outdated beliefs that influence our decisions regarding our children. Be mindful of this when your parents question your reasons for doing something.

It means that you, too, can change your beliefs about yourself. You, too, can believe that you CAN do something, that you are good enough.

When it comes to many things in life, it's a good idea to take a closer look at your values so that you can live authentically as you. It can be difficult with so many outside influences, especially friends, but it's fundamental to discover who you are and who you want to be.

So, how do you go about discovering your values? I do this with all the young people I work with, and here is an exercise you can complete to do just that.

VALUES EXCERCISE

1. Write a list of everything important to you, e.g. family, friendship, kindness, integrity, honesty, learning, money, success, well-being, giving back to the community, faith, and caring for yourself and others.

2. Narrow down your list to your three most important ones.

3. Write down why each of these three values is important to you.

4. Write down who you know who shares all three values.

5. Write down who you know who shares at least two of these values.

6. Give an example of how you live by each of your chosen values.

   If you're not already living by these three values, how can you make the necessary changes to include these in your everyday life? Are you living by these values in some parts of your life and not others?

If you're not already living by these three values, how can you make the necessary changes to include these in your everyday life? Are you living by these values in some parts of your life and not others?

BELIEFS

Now you've worked out those all-important values to live your life by, let's take a look at the beliefs that you've picked up along the way so far from parents, teachers, sports coaches, your peers and even social media (more on this later in a later chapter). Then let's see if they're ones you'd like to carry forward or whether they're ones you think should be left behind. You can do this exercise with a parent or other trusted adult if you want, as it will support you in opening up what can otherwise be a difficult conversation. You never know; it may even help them to let go of some old beliefs that are not serving them.

A great example of belief change has to be with a young client that I worked with, who had a strong belief that he would never amount to anything, that he would end up in prison, or even worse. He had found himself in a situation where he had taken on this belief, which had become his entire identity. He had been told time and time again that he was no good. He even told me that it was just the way he was and there was nothing he could do about it. His belief was so strong that he could see no other way. We got to work with the values and beliefs exercise, and before long, he was able to see that he could change. He had a choice; he could leave these beliefs behind and adopt new ones that would support him to become the person he truly wanted to be.

I asked him a different question. Instead of the all too familiar question 'what do you want to be when you get older?' you get asked all the time as a teenager, I asked him, 'WHO do you want to be?'

This was a question he freely admitted no one had ever asked him before and one that opened up a conversation that helped him realise that things didn't have to be this way. He wanted to be a business owner and a loving partner. He wanted kids and to be known as a good man.

As a result, he decided to make the necessary changes to create the life he wanted and not the life he had, up until that point, believed he deserved. Everyone deserves to be happy, lead a fulfilling life, be loved, feel safe and valued, and that includes you too.

When I was 15, I developed a belief I carried around for years. It came about when I was picked to do the 800 metres on our school sports day. I had always been good at this distance, so I was the natural choice for this event. We practised over and over in PE, and soon it became apparent that I was in with a strong chance of winning. I was small when I was at school, and gymnastics was my main sport, but I was happy that I could also show off my talents on the track. I was up against a few longer-legged students, so as a shorty, I was ready to prove that I could do it and that we short girls can run just as well as our taller friends.

The day of the event arrived. It was a hot, sunny day and the 800 metres was the last event. I had already run in the relay and was ready, confident, and feeling good about it.

The whistle blew, and off we went. The crowd was cheering, and I could hear teammates shouting my name and getting behind me. I was out in the lead for most of the race, and I was sure I would win. But then one of my longer-legged friends, who was my main competition, seemed to come out of nowhere in the last 200 metres and bam! She overtook me and carried on getting further away from me. I could hear my teammates still shouting, only now they sounded annoyed. They were shouting not-so-nice things at me, and at that moment, my new belief about myself kicked in. I started to believe that I couldn't run. I carried this belief with me until I was in my 40s. I would tell myself I couldn't run. I would make fun of people who ran, and this was all because I had created something in my head that suited me at that moment. Losing that race knocked my confidence and belief in myself. I chose the idea that I couldn't run to protect myself to ensure that the embarrassment of losing in front of my whole year at school never happened again.

The belief I created wasn't real or true, but I had made losing the evidence I needed to confirm it. Once I challenged this belief and the evidence I had created, I could find more evidence of it not being real or true. Since then, I have been running 5-10k regularly, giving myself a more supportive statement.

SETTING HEALTHY BOUNDARIES

There is a third key element to consider and implement when on this journey: working out, communicating and sticking by your boundaries. Why are these important? Boundaries protect us from being manipulated, hurt or taken advantage of. They help you to set limits with other people. They allow you to communicate what is and what isn't okay and what

CHALLENGE YOUR BELIEFS EXCERCISE

Here's how you, too, can discover and challenge your current beliefs about yourself.

1. Write down one of your current beliefs about yourself.

2. Write down what you're currently telling yourself about this belief. Listen to your inner voice. What is it telling you?

3. Recognise that this is just a belief and not a 'fact.'

4. Challenge the belief
   - Is it real?
   - What evidence do you have to back up this belief?
   - What evidence do you have to dispel this belief?
   - Does this belief belong to you, or has someone else given it to you?
   - Does this belief hold you back or move you forward?
   - What better belief can you create to support yourself from this day forward?

5. Write down your new, more supporting belief and put it somewhere you will see it daily.

6. Read it aloud to yourself at least ten times a day.

7. Take action and start implementings things that support your new belief.

you're uncomfortable with in any relationship. I include your relationship with yourself in this.

Boundaries will allow you to let people know how you'd like to be treated and can help to create space between you and others when needed. Establishing your boundaries comes after working on your values and beliefs; once known, these three things combined can be your compass for life. They will support you to know who you are, what is important to you and what you will and won't allow into your life.

This process can help you recognise your feelings and limits and enable you to communicate more effectively with friends, family, partners, colleagues and other people. It's important to ensure that you're setting both physical and emotional boundaries healthily. Remember, they're here to be your compass; they're not here to get your own way or for you to take advantage of other people. You must communicate them respectfully.

Setting boundaries is a way of standing up for yourself. But to do that and be accepted by those around you, you must communicate those boundaries. I meet so many young people who want to enforce boundaries, yet they don't share them with the necessary people, or they do so in a rude manner which only makes things worse.

Take, for example, a situation at school with a teacher. You may decide that you want to be spoken to/not spoken to in a certain way. Now you know this as it's something you have thought about and are clear about in your head. However, your teacher is not a mind reader. Although you think it's a

given that they should be respectful when they speak to you, you communicate in a rather rude manner when spoken to in a way that you deem unacceptable. This happens because your boundary has been crossed, which triggers your aggressive tone and a reaction to not communicating this boundary beforehand when you're feeling calm.

Another example could be within your friendship group where one friend is always speaking to you unkindly, which you feel is unacceptable. Yet, you've not talked to them about it in the past, so they continue to do it. Although this shouldn't be happening in the first place, you've never said anything to her, so she assumes it's okay. Yet, inside, it makes you feel angry, frustrated, and even self-conscious. In this instance, a healthy boundary to install here would be to speak to your friend away from the others and let her know how this makes you feel. Then ask her to please stop. If she continues to do it, you know she's likely to be doing it to get a reaction. In which case is she really a friend at all? Does this friendship meet with your values and beliefs? There will be more on this in the chapter about relationships later on.

You may have heard the expression' respect is earnt and not given.' It is very true, and it's also a two-way street. The best way to gain respect is to show respect, which includes being respectful of yourself. This is where setting healthy boundaries can help you achieve that. It's also a good idea to model the boundaries you wish to receive. Such as wanting to be spoken to a certain way. Suppose you talk to others with respect and kindness; you live through those all-important values you have set, but you're also teaching others how you want to be treated. You see, it is true that what you put out comes back to you. By modelling your own values, beliefs and boundaries towards others, you are actually attracting those back into your own life.

Take a moment to think about where you may need to set some healthy boundaries in your life. When you become frustrated, angry or stressed, is there a boundary issue at play at that moment? Do you need to reflect on your reaction and behaviour to see where that boundary may be being crossed and where you may be crossing another person's boundary? For example - your parents are likely to have set some boundaries for you, such as being home at a particular time and ringing if you're going to be late. Your parents want you to be safe at all times, so they implement these boundaries to support your safety, not because they want to make life as difficult for you as possible or are just being strict. So when you cross this boundary, you most likely get a frustrated, angry or stressed reaction from them.

When you find yourself in an uncomfortable situation, the likelihood is that what's happening goes against your values and beliefs or crosses one of your physical or emotional boundaries. Think back to when this happened and ask yourself, 'what was happening? Why did it feel uncomfortable?' See what boundary was being crossed and how you could communicate it in the future, so it doesn't happen again.

I think it's really important to say that how you communicate is crucial to the outcome you receive. As with anything in life, it's not always what you say; it's how you say it. If you speak with respect and positive language, you are always more likely to see a positive result.

Some examples of healthy boundaries are: Asking your parents or siblings to knock before entering your room. Ask your friends not to interrupt you when you're speaking. Tell a partner that you're comfortable with kissing, but not when your parents are in the room. Remember what I said about modelling these behaviours, so knock before entering your parent's or sibling's room. Don't interrupt people when they're speaking; ask your partner what they're comfortable and not comfortable with.

Always when doing these things, take some time for self-reflection and self-compassion. We are all a work in progress, and no one expects you to get everything right all the time, so don't be too hard on yourself and accept that you may fail a few times before you succeed. Any change and growth requires time and effort, but once you've committed yourself, you will start to see and feel the benefits.

If you don't do any of the other exercises in this book, please do these three as they have been known to create serious positive change and will stand you in good stead for your whole life. It's not just you that benefits, but the people around you do too. The ripple effect of this can be incredible. Sharing these exercises with your parents can support change for everyone.

CREATE HEALTHY BOUNDARIES EXCERCISE

1. Here's a simple 7-step process you can follow to set up healthy boundaries with those around you.

2. Review your values and beliefs exercises and look at what's important to you.

3. Work out where in your life you need to set boundaries.

4. Communicate those boundaries respectfully.

5. Reinforce the boundary when needed.

6. Stick with it - people try to push back when you first create boundaries as they won't understand or like that they're there, but they'll get used to them, so keep going.

7. Re-evaluate your boundaries now and then check if they're still relevant or if they need tweaking.

8. Self-reflect to see where you may be crossing boundaries and re-adjust where necessary.

9. Repeat these steps whenever the need arises.

CHAPTER SEVEN

RELATIONSHIPS

PARENTS/CARERS

The very first relationship you ever formed was with your parents/carer, and this relationship is the basis of how you form any other relationship in life. So if you had at least one loving parent or carer in those infant years, then you are likely to be able to build healthy relationships in one form or another. In some cases, however, where a parent has been absent, this can cause different attachment issues in later life. When I talk about absence, this doesn't just apply to those who aren't physically there. Due to their upbringing, some parents who are physically available can also be emotionally unavailable, making it more difficult for you to feel their love and support as a child.

To be emotionally unavailable refers to someone unable to communicate their feelings or deal with the emotions of others and therefore struggle to support others with their emotional needs.

Suppose your dad was absent either physically or emotionally. In that case, you may develop unhealthy relationships with men. If mum was absent, female friendships might be trickier for you to navigate.

That's not to say that this happens in every situation, but it is seen more as a general rule. Having said that, there are other reasons you may struggle in relationships, which could be due to other adult influences in early life.

A young girl came to me as she struggled with relationships with boys. She'd had a couple of brief boyfriends but found that she was attracting the same type of boy repeatedly. These boys were not treating her particularly well. They would ignore her messages and only respond when it suited them. They would make her feel like she was a possession to be ordered about. They were unable to respond appropriately to her emotional needs. She felt she was giving more love and support than they were prepared to give her. She admitted to being very jealous and of giving too much of herself to hope that they would respond and give her the affection and love she was craving. When we delved deeper into her early years, we discovered that her dad had left when she was small and had been absent for many of her younger years.

Once she became aware of the first time she felt not being good enough, not feeling loved and not being wanted, she could see the pattern she had been repeating with the boys she was attracted to. These boys were emotionally unavailable, just like her dad had been for her. She initially felt sad, and it took a while to come to terms with this. But after a few more sessions, some self-compassion and acceptance, she was able to work on attracting the type of boys that could give her the love and affection she now knew she deserved.

Your parents and carers significantly impact your life. When they are the type to show you unconditional love and affection, you have well and truly hit the jackpot. Now I know that in your teenage years, you feel like they don't get you and look at you like you just landed from outer space, but their number one concern for you is your safety. To know that you are okay, that you're looking after yourself and that you don't end up hurt physically or emotionally. Us parents would rather take all that pain into ourselves than watch you struggle in any way.

However, your parents will get things wrong from time to time. When their bundle of joy arrived, they weren't given a handbook on how to raise a child. The only way they knew to raise a child was the way their parents raised them. Their parents raised them the way their parents raised them, too, so you can see a generational cycle of parenting going on. But what parents find difficult to understand is that you are NOT growing up in the same society as they did.

Let's look at how your grandparents were raised. They may have gone to war or been the child of someone at war. They may have lived on little food, clothing and money in those times. Parents would have been away for months at a time, and they wouldn't always know where their next meal was coming from. Their parents raised them in a time of 'lack,' yet here you are being raised in a time of 'abundance.' You can have almost any food delivered to your door in half an hour and the latest gadgets the next day.

You live in a new age that no one else has lived through before. Your parents went out with friends, and no one knew where they were until dinner time. The time to be home was when the street lamps went on. Their parents couldn't track them on their phones. They had to trust that they would be okay and that they would be home on time.

Times have changed, and we find ourselves in an age where parents have developed a habit of over-parenting. Yes, I said it. Parents are now over-parenting their children. Why? Because they can - the technology is available. The knowledge and fear are there for all to see on the news, social media and live streaming on platforms such as YouTube.

So, the next time they ask you where you're going, who with and all the other questions they bombard you with, take a minute to consider all the things they now know that their parents didn't know about the world you're growing up in. They're not doing it to be annoying, no matter how much it sounds and feels like they are. They're not doing it to be a party pooper or the fun police! They ask because they care and because you're still their world, no matter how old or tall you are.

If, for some reason, you feel like they're being unreasonable with their boundaries around you going out, etc., and you'd like more autonomy and freedom, sit them down and explain that you understand they're worried. You know the world you're growing up in is different, but let them know that you understand this world a little better than they do as you've grown up in it. Reach a compromise with them. And most importantly, if you make an alternative suggestion to the one they do, make sure you stick to it. Your parents want to be able to trust you; once you break that trust, it isn't easy to regain it. This approach will save a lot of door slamming and arguments and even bring you closer again if you've been feeling a little disconnected from them of late.

FRIENDSHIPS

Female friendships are complicated. There's no way around it. If you haven't had the best role model in your childhood, navigating teenage friendships with your girlfriends can be an even bigger minefield. Most girls have had their mum or female carer to guide them on how to forge healthy friendships. But others may have witnessed friendships that could be considered toxic. Still, having seen these from a young age, you could be mistaken for thinking this is the norm. The possibility of copying these patterns is relatively high, although not a given. You may have been able to see through those friendships for what they are and decided not to follow this example.

I had a young girl work with me who had a strained relationship with her mum and had always thought that her mum had favoured her brother. More on siblings later. She had developed some friendships that were causing her high levels of stress and anxiety. This was due to their nature of intensity and the friendships feeling one-sided and controlling. She was acting out of character and doing things that she wouldn't ordinarily entertain, let alone do. She was starting to feel lost and confused. We started her with the three key elements. We worked out her values, let go of her old beliefs around her relationship with her mum and created some boundaries to support her to take back a little control over what was happening in her friendships. Soon she became more confident and more assertive and realised that these particular friends were not friends at all.

You grow a lot through those secondary years, and as you do so, some of your values will change, as will your interests.

You are likely to shift friendship groups at least once or even twice through school, which is okay. In year seven, you may be into dance or football. Yet, by year ten, you may have begun to be more interested in hair and beauty or even mechanics, in which case you will naturally gravitate to people who share those same interests and those who no longer share the same interests may drift away and make other friendships.

There will be a point, though, when you may feel isolated as you transition from one group to another. This is perfectly normal and completely okay. Every young girl I speak to has been in this position. I, too, felt isolated during year nine when a friendship group of mine decided that I no longer fit into what they considered to be 'cool' status. At the time, I was devastated. I found myself alone at lunchtime, wondering how I would survive the next two years at school if I had no solid friendship unit to call my own. Then one day when I was in the canteen a girl asked me where I got my bag from, and we chatted as we ate lunch. That girl then introduced me to her friends who also loved my bag, and from that day forward, we hung around together and stayed friends for years to come.

We did everything together, had the best last two years of school, and had much fun - more fun than I ever had with the other group. That group ended up all falling out and being nasty to each other, so I was glad to be out of that. As someone who believes these things happen for a reason, it's clear that I ended up better off than they did. I look back now and thank them for rejecting me because I didn't belong there, even though I felt like the world was caving in when it happened. Instead, the world was looking after me and supporting me to grow and expand.

If you're finding yourself in a similar situation and you doubt if your friends are really the ones for you, go back to your values and ask yourself who in that group shares all three and at least two. If only one or two of them share your values, then it might be time to re-think and seek out those who show more interest in your interests and who value your friendship as much as you do theirs.

Remember, if you're not communicating or modelling what you expect from a friendship, you can't be surprised if you're not in alignment with it. Mind reading doesn't work here or in any other relationship, for that matter. If a friend is acting in a way that you're not comfortable with, for example, if they're speaking unkindly about another friend behind their back or being mean to someone in front of you, pull them to one side. Then explain that you're not comfortable and why, and if they are a real friend, they will listen and respond in a compassionate and understanding way.

No friendship is perfect, and we all make mistakes. Seeking the perfect friendship is only going to cause disappointment. We're human beings, not robots. Emotional projection plays a huge part in female relationships, and we all see in each other some of the things we are unhappy with within ourselves. You may criticise a friend who you feel has more than you or is prettier than you. You won't come out and say it, though, as it's deep down in your subconscious mind, which is like a big library where you store all of your past experiences. You'll start by making small digs at her

HEALTHY FRIENDSHIPS EXCERCISE

1. Here are a few tips on how to work out if a friendship is a keeper or not.
2. What do you want from your friendship?
3. Are you getting those things from this particular friend?
4. What don't you want from this friendship?
5. Is this current friend showing any of these things within the friendship?
6. What do you value in a friend?
7. Does this friend share those values?
8. Do you feel comfortable around this person?
9. Are you able to discuss things with this person?
10. Are you happy to remain in the friendship, having answered the above questions?

and then maybe inadvertently get others to agree with you to validate how you feel. People who are hurting hurt others. Remember that, too, and be aware of when you're not being kind, as it could indicate that you need to pay attention to something that is going on for you. Maybe you're not feeling great about something within yourself or something that has happened, and to make you feel better, you take it out on a friend or vice versa.

There will be times when you disagree with your friends, and that's okay. They won't always agree with you. It's when things start to get uncomfortable and out of alignment with who you are and who you want to be that it's time to re-think the friendship.

SIBLINGS

Did you know that most young people suspect a sibling is their parent's favourite child? So if you have a sibling, chances are you think they're the favourite, yet they think you're the favourite. Having spoken to my sister about this not long ago, I realised that this was true for us as she had thought I was the favourite, yet I felt she was the favourite. This goes back to our unique maps of the world and how we experience life from an early age.

You may have found that when you and your sibling or siblings were young, you got on really well, played together and had each other's back on the playground, but things are very different now. You no longer see eye to eye and argue about pretty much everything. A sibling who you once considered to be your best friend is now this annoying little alien species who keeps hanging around and being

embarrassing. Sometimes you want them to disappear to have peace, quiet, and privacy.

I get it. I used to be that annoying younger sister, and to be fair, it's our job to embarrass our older siblings in front of their friends and boyfriends even more so. Your teenage years are a time of much change inside and outside yourself. You become more self-aware, and your self-doubt becomes heightened as you feel the need to fit in and belong. Yet there is your younger sibling reminding you daily that your hair looks rubbish, you've got too much make-up on, or you've got a bogey hanging down from your nose, and not quietly either. It feels like they want the whole world to know to cause you the most embarrassment possible. And then if you have an older sibling, they're there to tell you how to do everything and how not to do something because they know EVERYTHING and you know nothing! It's no wonder that some days you want to shut yourself in your room and pretend none of them exist, or you want to spend more time at friends' houses because at least there, you can watch your friend being embarrassed instead.

All of this makes you feel self-conscious and start to over think things and look at yourself differently. While all this is happening, you begin projecting how you feel about yourself onto them. The parts you no longer like about yourself become the ammunition to fire back at them. For instance, you feel like your brother or sister is a goody goody and your parents favour them over you. You think you're always the one getting into trouble, so you project that on to your sibling and start taking it out on them and being horrible and telling them how bad they are. You pick a fight with them so you can purposefully say horrible things to them to make yourself feel better.

By doing this, you can ignore your faults and put them on to others. Looking at our faults can be difficult. Accepting that you have these faults will further embed your belief if you already feel like you're not good enough. So instead, you put them into your external environment for others to pick up and possess, like your brother or sister.

Sibling rivalry is real and happens in all homes. If you become more aware of what's happening to you at that moment, it can support you to make a better decision about how you communicate with them. As humans, we are primarily conditioned to find fault in people. As you know your siblings inside out and have lived with them for so many years, it's no wonder the things you used to find cute about them have become annoying as you've grown older.

Now, I see perfectionism everywhere in the work that I do. I am an ex-perfectionist and have worked with many young girls who struggle with feeling not good enough for one reason or another. I want you to be clear that perfect doesn't actually exist. No relationship is perfect, no job is perfect, no school is perfect, no parent, friend or boyfriend is perfect, and neither are YOU, and THAT'S OKAY. Like everyone else, you and your family are a work in progress.

YOUR FIRST LOVE

Love is intense through your teenage years, and this will be the first one-to-one relationship you will have had outside of your family's safe and comforting love. With the need for approval and at a time when you're highly influenced by

what people think of you, your first love is a very important one. It's all about love and belonging, which everyone wants. Our human need for community is also a contributing factor when choosing your first partner.

You never forget your first love, even if they don't turn out to be The One, which is highly unlikely. Not many people stay with their childhood sweetheart. This first romantic relationship will teach you much. Not just about yourself but also about how you perceive love, how you want love to feel and, in some cases, how you don't want love to feel. Those first flutters of nerves when you see them or hear their voice. The feeling that you might burst every time you think about them and the constant smile on your face that other people can't miss. It's a knowing sign that you are in the dizzy heights of love.

I met my first love in year 10 of secondary school. He was such a lovely boy. He was kind, and we had great fun. On our first Valentine's Day, he rode to my house, a few miles from his home, early in the morning, about 5 am, to leave me some chocolates and a red rose on my doorstep. I was so flattered and felt so much love and appreciation for his gesture. At school, word got around about what he had done. Some girls at school were obviously jealous that their boyfriends had not done the same. They started bad-mouthing me and saying I didn't deserve such a lovely boyfriend because I hadn't gone all out for him. Some of the more popular girls tried to make me feel bad. They projected how they felt about their relationships onto me. Still, I didn't take any notice as both myself and Neil knew that he had completely surprised me and he loved what I got him.

I could have let those girls make me feel bad about myself. I could have believed that I hadn't deserved him or the gifts he gave me, but I could see how jealous they were, and that was enough for me at the time. I was never one for all the attention being on me, so I did feel some embarrassment about the situation, and for a moment, I doubted myself. With it being my first romantic relationship, I didn't know if those girls were right or not, but I stood by my convictions and let them get on with their envy.

There will always be people who won't be happy when you find your first love due to jealousy or fear of not finding anyone themselves. You may also find yourself jealous or fearing that you may lose a friend due to them spending more time with their partner. If you find yourself in this position, recognise that you are projecting your fear of being left behind, not fitting in, and belonging to anyone. Try not to let it overspill into how you support your friend in their relationship.

My first love was healthy and one that I learned a lot from. I learnt how I wanted to be treated and how to be truly grateful when someone showed me their love through their actions. But first loves are not always healthy. I recently worked with a young girl in an on/off relationship with a boy she had known for some years. They would be happy for a while, and then it would all go wrong and split up. He would then turn on her and become possessive. He wouldn't leave her alone and even involved her friends and family in his attempts to win her back. He would lie and bombard her with texts accusing her of talking to other boys and being out of order. He would even tell her what she had been doing

because he had people reporting to him. She had become concerned and didn't know which way to turn.

We talked at length about their first few months of love and how it had felt compared to how it felt now. We looked at how she wanted to be treated compared to how he was treating her, and we took a long look at why she felt she had to keep going back. This young girl believed that she didn't deserve anything better. That this relationship was the best, it was ever going to be for her.

Thankfully, she worked through this belief and recovered her self-worth and self-compassion. Then she could pull away and move on to a healthier relationship where she felt comfortable giving and receiving love with no conditions attached.

When you're young, and those first feelings of love are so intense, it's natural to feel deeply hurt when it ends. It can take a long time to move on from this, and it's okay for you to take that time to heal. This is likely the first time you've felt emotionally rejected, and it's a tough feeling to come back from. Taking a step back to work out what did and didn't work is totally alright. How you acted within the relationship and how they left you feeling. Every feeling you have when a relationship ends is valid, and we all heal differently.

This is one of my favourite exercises when things get rocky in any relationship. When you're finding it difficult to understand a situation between yourself and someone else, give the below NLP perspective technique a go. It's a great way to see things from another viewpoint. It's also a great one to teach your loved ones too.

PERSPECTIVE TECHNIQUE

Place 3 chairs in a circle.....

1. Sit in the first chair and think of a time when you disagreed with a friend, family member or teacher. Think back to how you felt and what was said. Sit here for a moment and remember it from your perspective.

2. Get up, move to the second chair, and put yourself in the other person's shoes. Go back to the disagreement and look at it through their eyes, as if you were them at that moment. Now think about how they felt and how they saw it. Sit with that for a moment.

3. Now get up and move to the third chair, where you will be a complete outsider looking in on the disagreement. What do you see happening between these two people? How do you think they could resolve things?

4. Write down anything you would do differently if you went back to that disagreement now that you have put yourself in the other person's shoes and seen it as an outsider.

5. Would you have dealt with things differently? What have you learnt that you could use the next time you find yourself in a similar situation?

YOUR RELATIONSHIP WITH YOURSELF

I cannot tell you how important this relationship is. It is undoubtedly the most important relationship you will ever have. As you grow and make your way in the world, you will meet many people, friends, partners, colleagues, and business associates and have different relationships with all of them. Some will come into your life and stay for a while. Some will come and go very quickly, and others will stay the distance, but there is only one person who will be with you the entire journey, and that is YOU!

Further on in this book is a whole chapter on 'About YOU.' Self-compassion, self-acceptance, self-care, self-esteem and more, so I'm not going to go into detail here. I just want you to know that you are important, you are worthy, you are enough, and you need to become your number one fan. True happiness comes from within. From how you see yourself so that you can shine, thrive and fulfil your true potential, no matter what you want your life to look like.

I know you're too hard on yourself. I see this all the time, and I know how that feels. I was exactly the same as a young girl. I grew up in an environment that expected a lot from me. I took on the identity that I needed to punish myself if I did something wrong, as I had been as a young child, if I didn't do well enough or didn't do what was asked of me when I was asked. I see this a lot, which is why I decided to write this book. I want every young girl to know that she is ENOUGH, no matter what. She is whole - whether she is tall, short, introverted, academic, practical, creative, sporty and everything else in between!

I'd like you to take a moment now to close your eyes and see yourself shine. See yourself as your happiest version. Feel how it feels, see how it looks and listen to what's happening around you in that image. Keep that image with you so you can pull on it when you need to when you start to doubt yourself. Create that happy place, as I call it. I do this with all my clients, and it's super useful to have a place to take yourself when things feel a little difficult. Then you can see clearly, feel calmer, and remind yourself that your goal to be happy is achievable as long as you keep tapping into yourself along the way.

CHAPTER EIGHT

THOUGHTS, EMOTIONS AND BEHAVIOUR

YOUR BRAIN AND HOW IT DEVELOPS

To understand your thoughts, emotions and behaviour better, it's important first to understand a little about your brain development.

This can be complex and scientific, but I will simplify it. Understanding how your brain works can support you not just now but throughout life. It's something I wish I'd learnt when I was a teenager. It took me a long time to get my head around it, and I don't want to lose you with the science.

By the time you were six years old, your brain was already just over 90% of its adult size. So as you can imagine, those early years were pretty crucial for your overall brain development. A lot was going on. Your brain was like a sponge, soaking up everything that was happening around you - every sound, smell, image, and touch. It was absorbing and framing your experiences. It supported you to grow, roll over, walk, talk, use a spoon, and work out feelings, both your own and those around you. It sounds a lot, doesn't it, when you think back to everything you learnt and experienced up until that age.

Things tend to slow down a little and level out after that. For a while anyway. But then the next big wave of development

arrives in your teenage years. This is where you primarily use the amygdala part of your brain, which is associated with emotions, aggression, impulses and risky behaviour. Yes, this is the part I really wish I'd known earlier. The pre-frontal cortex part of your brain, which supports you to plan, think about consequences, solve problems and control those impulses, is not fully formed yet and won't be until you're around 25! It's all starting to make a little more sense now, right?

In truth, your brain is still under construction and whilst this is happening, things seem confusing. One minute you may feel like you've got this thing called life all sussed out, and the next minute you feel overwhelmed with even the most basic stuff. You're still using the emotional side of your brain more than your logical side.

This isn't to say that you can use this as an excuse for inappropriate and over-risky behaviour. Things such as drinking, going somewhere you know you're not meant to be, starting arguments with people you meet when out and about or getting yourself into fights and saying, 'it's my brain development's fault!' It's not, but it does help you to understand better why you feel the way you do and how you can help yourself during this time of development.

On top of knowing about your development, it's helpful to know a little more about how you can hack your mind to create deeper learning, develop healthier habits and let go of unhealthy ones.

Your brain lies at the very centre of your nervous system and consists of billions of cells known as neurons. These fire together to create neural pathways; the more you use these pathways, the stronger that pathway becomes. So if you're learning something new, the neurons will fire together, linking together. Still, this pathway will be weak at first, but as you keep learning, it will become stronger. Once you know it, it will become even stronger and almost habitual, so you don't have to think too hard about it. It becomes pretty much automatic, which is how you can form healthy and unhealthy habits. The strength of this pathway can be why it's hard to break an unhealthy habit! But you can do it by creating a new pathway, but it needs to be done consistently over time. It's better to learn by doing something once a day for five consecutive days than by doing something five times in just one day.

Remember when you learnt to ride a bike? You repeatedly practised, and the neurons in your brain were firing together to create that path until it became so strong it was habitual. In time, every time you got on your bike, your brain knew exactly what to do, thanks to those neurons. The same happened when you learned to roll over, talk, walk, and eat with a spoon.

Your brain is a muscle, so just like working your leg and arm muscles by going to the gym to build them up, you need to train your brain and challenge it to grow. With this in mind, you can start to teach your brain to work for you rather than against you, and we call this a 'growth mindset,' which I'll be showing you how to do within this book.

THOUGHTS

Your thoughts are the words that you say to yourself inside your head. No one else hears the words unless you speak them out loud.

The biggest thing to remember about thoughts is - they are just thoughts. Thoughts are NOT facts. Sometimes your mind gets it wrong. It plays tricks on you. You can think that you're not good enough or pretty enough, or clever enough or that you can't do something, but actually, you are, and you can. Your mind is telling you that you're not or can't to try and protect you, as it's been programmed to do that over the years. Yet as you get older, you have a choice to make. Will you continue allowing your mind to tell you these things, or will you start taking some control over your thoughts and choosing better ones because you are the thinker of your thoughts?

We, humans, have, on average, between 40,000-70,000 thoughts every day. Sounds overwhelming, doesn't it? You may even be thinking right now about how that surely can't be possible. Well, it is; we don't notice so many of them because they are often drowned out by what's happening around us or other thoughts that may be newer. Those old thoughts that go around and around in our heads most of the time are now on automatic pilot, so they're in there and affecting our daily life. We're just not conscious of them anymore.

What if I told you that most of those daily thoughts are negative? They originate from stories others have told you in the past about yourself or that you've created for yourself. Stories like "I'm no good at Maths. I am bad at spelling. I can't do difficult things, or there's no point even trying as I know I can't do it". Society conditions us for survival, and back in the caveman days, when there was danger everywhere, our first thoughts were how to survive, look out for danger, and fight. We don't live like that anymore, but our brains are still primed for survival.

The good news is that you get to choose your thoughts. It's been scientifically proven that you can change your thoughts about yourself and others thanks to the amazing plasticity in your brain. It allows you the capacity to adapt and change as a result of your experiences. So you can turn "I'm no good at maths" into "I have the basics, and I'm working towards understanding the more difficult stuff" or "there's no point even trying" into "I can do difficult things when I put my mind to it and give it a go."

Here is one way in which you can catch your thoughts as they come up and start to re-frame them into more positive ones when needed.

Let's put your thoughts to the test. Let's see if they are indeed FACT or NOT.

THOUGHTS ON TRIAL EXERCISE

In this exercise, you will be putting a thought on trial as if in a courtroom. You will be the defence lawyer, the prosecution and the judge to determine the accuracy of the thought.

The defence lawyer and the prosecution will gather evidence for and against the thought. This evidence can only be used if it is indeed FACT. No interpretations, guesses or opinions. Finally, the judge will come to a verdict on the thought. You will then ask yourself if the thought is accurate and fair. Are there other thoughts that are closer to the facts?

THOUGHTS ON TRIAL EXERCISE

1. Write down the thought or thoughts you're having.
2. Become the defence lawyer and write down all the evidence your mind has for the thought.
3. Become the prosecution lawyer and write down all the evidence against the thought.
4. Be the judge and give your verdict on whether the thought is accurate, fair and factual.

This is a third-person perspective NLP technique (details on NLP can be found in the resources at the back of this book) that is very powerful and can be used for any thoughts you have.

You get to choose your thoughts, so let your inner judge step forward and take this opportunity to be your own teacher in this. You can even imagine one of your own teachers in your mind. It could be the teacher who points and wags their fingers in class, the teacher who looks down his nose at you, or the one who pulls the silliest faces when they're not impressed with a class member. Use their voice and expressions to give your negative thoughts a good talking to. Feel free to have a little fun with this to help you work through things.

Here are a few other ways that you can support your teenage mind.

GRATITUDE

Practising daily gratitude is another good way to change your thinking patterns to more positive ones. Write down three things that you are grateful for each day. Start small, and with practice, you will be able to notice these things as and when they appear. This, too, will become an automatic thought pattern that will better support you both now and in the future.

MEDITATION

You can also use meditation effectively to bring your thoughts into your awareness and recognise the emotions attached.

BODY SCAN MEDITATION

Get yourself into a comfortable position where you won't be disturbed. Close your eyes and take three slow, deep breaths in and out whilst imagining that your whole body is warm and surrounded by a beautiful yellow light. Imagine the relaxing feeling of the warm sunshine on your body.

Now start to think about your body, looking for any tense areas that are not feeling relaxed. Focus on those parts of your body for a moment and feel the sensations coming up.

If they feel tense, consciously relax them and move on to the next part of your body that is feeling tense.

Once you've done that, bring your focus to the top of your head and your face. Can you feel any sore or tense areas here? If yes, take a deep breath in and relax those areas as you breathe out.

Next, move to the neck and shoulders and really focus on these common tense areas. Do you feel any tension here? If yes, take another deep breath in and relax this area as you breathe out again.

Move your focus to your tummy and back. Notice how you're feeling, take a deep breath and relax these areas as you breathe out.

Do the same with your legs and repeat down your body until you reach your feet and toes. Wriggle your toes and make sure that your feet are relaxed. Take another deep breath in and relax your whole body as you breathe out.

Repeat twice before opening your eyes and noticing how much more relaxed you now feel.

Bringing your awareness back to your body will ease any stress and worry you may carry.

A teenage girl was referred to me after her mum had noticed that she was talking more negatively about herself. After our second session together, we discovered that her thoughts around the size of her nose had started when someone commented about her to some of her friends; they then started commenting. She had developed a negative thought pattern about her appearance, a typical pattern amongst teenage girls. Until then, she had always come across as a pretty confident girl.

As a result, she got into a negative thought loop and told herself that what they were saying must be true. We re-framed, and she realised that other people's thoughts and opinions are not facts. Neither are our thoughts, and the friends were likely to be projecting their insecurities about themselves onto her. She could see how her thought pattern had spiralled and got stuck in a cycle of lies.

Cognitive distortions are those irrational thoughts that we have that often influence our emotions. We all experience these to a degree, and here is how you can recognise some of the more common ones.

All-or-nothing thinking - Also known as black and white thinking, is often used by those who see anything other than perfection as a failure, e.g. I didn't get the grade I was

predicted, so I must be stupid. Or, I didn't get on the team last time, so what's the point of trying again?

Mind reading - You assume you know what someone else is thinking about you or another person or situation. When actually, you made it up in your mind without asking them what they're really thinking. Giving yourself false information, e.g. I'm speaking to my friend, and she isn't listening. She obviously doesn't like me anymore and thinks I'm boring (the truth is that she has a big test coming up and is distracted, which is nothing to do with you at all).

Over-generalisation - When you broaden a belief about one thing to create the same belief about something else. For instance, you feel awkward in an interview and then believe you always feel awkward.

Disqualification of the positive - You tend to ignore the positive outcome or experience, favouring the negative one. Often used to reconfirm a negative belief about yourself or a situation. Most likely to keep you safe in your known and comfortable old belief pattern.

Catastrophising - Blowing a thought or experience up to be bigger than its reality, e.g. If I fail this exam, I will end up in a dead-end job all my life.

If you notice yourself doing any of these, use the above exercise to put those thoughts on trial.

EMOTIONS

Your emotions are linked to your thoughts which are also

linked to how you behave. When you're a baby, you primarily show emotion through crying. Believe it or not, as a baby, you will have had different tones to your cry to communicate your needs. Whether that be hunger, tiredness, tummy ache, pain of any kind or sadness. You would have smiled to show happiness. Then as you become a toddler, you will have learnt how to express some of those emotions differently. Typically happiness or sadness. Some of these will have been taught by your caregivers at home, in pre-school or in play groups. You will have witnessed other toddlers expressing their frustration and anger by throwing things and their happiness through shouting and screaming with joy.

You will have noticed, though, that as you enter your pre-teen years, your emotions are heightened in many ways, and you may no longer feel in control of them as they become more intense. It's believed that this 'big emotions' stage runs between the ages of 10 and 16, with particularly high levels between ages 13 and 15. You might be nodding as you read this, thinking, 'yep, that sounds about right.' You may even be able to relate this to a sibling or friend. You won't necessarily hit this stage simultaneously as your friends. You may enter this earlier or later, and you may even glide through this time, but it's a good guide to go by and helps you understand yourself and others better.

I work with young people who are in varying stages, but the one thing I notice in all of them is that they are struggling to self-regulate and understand why it's happening. I see a lot of frustration overspill into anger and a lot of confusion overspill into shame and guilt because they're unable to articulate in what we adults consider to be an appropriate manner. They

don't feel like they are being seen or heard for who they are as an individual, which is another reason for writing this book.

SELF-REGULATION

Self-regulation is a skill people learn to manage their emotions and behaviours in difficult situations. If you've not been given support in co-regulation as a young child, particularly from the primary caregiver, self-regulation, as you get older, will be more difficult. However, it's never too late to learn. Don't forget that your rational thinking mind is not yet fully constructed. You're still using your emotional mind for most things that will enhance those big feelings.

However, through the teenage years, there are so many new emotions stepping forward that it can be hard to recognise them as they arise. Let's take love, for example. Now, this is a deep emotion that means different things to different people. Until now, love has been unconditional for the most part. You've got your friendships which have a deep connection, but when you start a romantic relationship, love shifts into a whole new gear! And navigating and knowing how to react, respond or generally behave around this feeling can be alien and intense, meaning you may act differently from how you may have done before. You may not recognise this new behaviour which can heighten other emotions such as fear and frustration.

So, what are some new emotions you may feel: Anger, frustration, shame, guilt, stress, fear, love, happiness, or excitement?

All of these emotions are okay to feel. You need to feel

ALL of them, not just in your mind but in your body. Your emotions show up in your body and can become buried deep if you don't address them. They can cause health issues such as migraines, digestive problems, high blood pressure, or chronic pain in muscles and joints. When you have an unpleasant emotion, you naturally want to fight it, push it down or away, but all too often, this actually makes things worse. You've probably seen a friend or family member get angry over something that seems really small, and you'll think they've overreacted. Well, that's generally because their anger has been sitting within them for a while. It might have been a build-up of more minor anger mixed in with some frustration, stress and fear of a few different situations that weren't felt or dealt with at the moment, and this blow-up is a result of that. Their anger and frustration can turn into self-criticism and negative self-talk, making them feel worse and becoming a vicious circle of negative emotions.

Another example is if you're feeling anxious about a test or exam, you might start to worry about how that anxiety will impact the outcome of your test or exam. You may begin to fear and fight the anxious feeling, which will probably make you feel even more nervous. However, if you allow the feeling to flow through your body, feel where it's sitting and delay a reaction so that you can respond to the feeling, you will naturally calm down.

Your emotions are trying to tell you something, as is the behaviour it triggers. They can be the result of a thought, which, remember, is not automatically fact, or from something someone has said or done. You may feel sad because a friend didn't keep their word about meeting up.

You start to think they don't like you anymore, which triggers further sadness and negative behaviour, such as taking it out on your other friend, your parents or sibling.

Listen to your emotions, feel where they are in your body, and allow them to pass through you instead of reacting to them. Your emotions flow through your mind and body and are then released, but only if you allow them. Trust me, this takes practice and self-regulation in tough times is not something that happens overnight, and even then, you'll still get it wrong at times. This may bring on shame or guilt emotions as a result. This was a big one for me. I spent many years feeling guilty and shameful for not being enough in one way or another. Holding on to those emotions caused mental and physical pain and dictated how I lived my life for many years. I attracted the wrong people into my life who didn't share any of my values but who I thought I deserved to be around. They topped up my shame and guilt bucket repeatedly until I discovered that I could take back control of these emotions. I found out how to allow them to surface and face them in the moment, and here are a few things I did that I'd like to share with you.

MINDFULNESS

I started using Mindfulness to bring me back to the present moment, learn to live in the here and now, and thank my past for the lessons it taught me. I learnt not to worry about the things I can't control, and I started to look to the future but still live in the now.

VISUALISATIONS

I used visualisations to accept, allow and let go of the negative emotions that kept me in survival mode and the stress response. Putting my imagination to good use with positive thinking allowed me to see how to release these emotions. I learnt to love myself for who I am, not what others see me as being, not as others expect me to be, but for ME. I learnt to be ME. Introverted, empathetic, sensitive at times, kind and compassionate. I stopped comparing myself to others because no one else can be me, and that's a good thing, not a bad one.

There is a great letting go exercise you can do for this in chapter 9

I use the body scan meditation mentioned earlier in this chapter to pick up on where I'm feeling a particular emotion. I allow the feelings and sensations to flow and talk my body back down into a calm state. I let my thoughts float past in my mind and recognise any patterns that might be emerging. I have learnt to respond rather than react in difficult situations.

What you put out comes back to you in all aspects of life. I started practising gratitude which you can find in chapter 11 each day to create more positive emotions in my daily life.

- If you want respect, show respect.
- If you want love, give love.
- If you want kindness, give kindness.
- If you show gratitude, you will receive gratitude and so on!

YOUR BEHAVIOUR IS THE MESSAGE

'Don't shoot the messenger' is an old saying but one that is so true regarding behaviour. Yours or other people's

behaviour is your body and mind's way of letting you know something isn't right. A need isn't being met, a boundary has been crossed, or you may not be acting according to your values.

Those big emotions may be responding to a thought, or a thought may be responding to an emotion that feels like it's come out of nowhere. All behaviour has a positive message that needs to be listened to, but some behaviours are negative and inappropriate and can even be dangerous at times. So you must watch out for those behaviours, and if they become the norm for you, then it may be time to talk through your thoughts and feelings with a trusted adult.

I worked with a young lad whose behaviour pattern had become deeply rooted in his identity. He had become known for his aggression towards anyone who confronted him. This behaviour was causing him problems in school, at home and when he was out and about. He told me that this was just who he was and that he couldn't do anything about it. He had developed the belief that he could not change it, that he was made this way and that any attempt to address it was useless. He found it hard to trust people, but after a while, he felt comfortable enough to open up about some of his early childhood years. There had been a particular incident that first triggered this feeling of anger. Since then, every time he was confronted, this feeling was activated again and he would behave in the same way. He looked at all the triggers and realised that anger is not who he is; it doesn't define him. It's an emotion he has felt for similar reasons throughout his childhood. He could see a different way and learned to respond rather than react.

This didn't happen overnight, and he had a few 'blips' along the way, but we focused on what he got right each time and how he could change things next time. He was always being hard on himself whenever he got it wrong again. Still, by showing himself more compassion and accepting that he is human and not a robot, he has been letting go of a lot of the shame he was carrying around who he was. He knows he's not perfect, and he knows that it's okay. He now has better control over his big emotions and says he carries me around in his head, and when faced with this emotion, he asks himself, 'what would Faye say to me right now?'

Your thoughts, emotions and behaviour are all linked. They can be a healthy or unhealthy cycle and become a healthy habit or an unhealthy one. One quick way of breaking this cycle is to look at each part when you notice yourself behaving a certain way and ask yourself why this is happening. What is it telling me? What can I do to change things? Who can help me with this?

Here is an example of the thought, emotions, and behaviour loop that I see when I first start working with people, and this doesn't just go for young people. When people see the missing link in this loop, it helps them to interrupt their own loop so they can see it in more context.

Thought - I think X doesn't like me. Your mind flicks through the library of thoughts to find another thought to back up this one.

Emotion - I feel sad as I feel left out. Perhaps you are feeling left out somewhere else and feeling the same in this

situation too. Your mind taps into the emotional file to find more evidence to back up this emotion.

Behaviour - You pull away from that person and others to back up the thoughts and feelings. You end up feeling more left out, which backs up your thoughts and feelings on this situation.

So let's try to interrupt this cycle by challenging the process and adding a further step to rebalance your emotional mind with your rational mind.

Reality - is the thought you have a fact? Is it real? When else have you felt like this? Are the two feelings related? Are you behaving in a way that creates more of what you're feeling instead of solving the problem?

When you notice a friend or loved one's negative behaviour, they may need a little extra help or support, so you could try to ask them if they need anything. If they're finding something challenging, offer them an empathic ear so they can offload. You can even do the above exercise with them to help them explore what's going on and find the reality of what's happening so they can solve the problem.

Sometimes interrupting a thought or emotion is all that's needed, and doing the above will help you to achieve that.

CHAPTER NINE

It's All About YOU!

Have you ever been told, "it's not all about you, you know!"

Well, actually, it is.

Self-compassion, self-love, self-esteem, self-confidence, self-acceptance, and self-belief. It all starts with YOU!

As a young girl, I had no idea how to give myself any of these after being bullied aged ten by my gymnastics coach, who used me as an example of how not to do things. He always called me out on the things I was doing wrong and told all the other girls how useless he thought I was. He expressed how I shouldn't be there and that I was only there because my mum was friends with one of the other coaches. A grown man was openly bullying a ten-year-old girl. Yet, I didn't have the confidence to stand up for myself at the time. I just stood there and listened as he belittled me repeatedly.

As a result, I became pretty withdrawn, and my confidence and self-esteem plummeted. As for believing that I was good enough, you can forget it. Every week it embedded a belief in me that I was not good enough, which stayed with me for many years.

I see this too in many of the young people I work with, whereby teachers, coaches and peers have told them that

they aren't good enough for one reason or another. Maybe they don't understand what to do, they don't easily grasp grammar, they don't see things the same way, or they're not the same as their siblings or friends. Regardless of the circumstances, others have made them feel guilty, shameful, fearful or embarrassed of who they are.

As someone who carried shame and guilt around for all those years, I can see very quickly where young people are doing the same. It's so important that you understand how unique and worthy you are despite what other people say about you and what they try to convince you to believe about yourself.

SELF-COMPASSION

Showing self-compassion can seem a little cringy when you initially start to practice it, and self-love may feel totally alien. After all, if you've ever heard someone say, 'look at her, she loves herself,' you're going to believe that loving yourself is a bad thing, right? Well, actually, it's crucial. But I mean in a way that aligns with your values and who you really are. To stop constantly comparing yourself to others, you need to stop looking outside of yourself and what others have and what you haven't. Look within to find your true uniqueness and embrace it, accept it and love all your parts.

I worked with a young girl recently who was very body conscious. She was always talking very negatively about herself and saying that other people looked better than her and had better legs, a better bum and a flatter tummy. She was so busy focusing on what they had that she was missing the good things that she had too. So we set to work flipping her focus onto what she had to be grateful for in general and then moved on to feeling thankful for all the parts of her body and thanking them for everything they do for her daily. She thanked her legs for being strong and healthy and holding her up. She thanked her bum for allowing her to sit comfortably when she needed to, and she appreciated her tummy for enabling her to store the organs required to enjoy the delicious food she ate. Having a new appreciation for what her body did for her helped her stop comparing it to other people and allowed her to view herself more positively. I asked her to write a note on her mirror that she could read every morning, saying, "I love you".

Your teenage years are challenging, with much physical and emotional change. I see so many of you being ultra-hard on yourselves, so show yourself more compassion daily. You're human; you're going to get things wrong, just like younger children and adults do. You're growing and learning along the way, so remind yourself of that and go a little easier on yourself.

Regularly practising self-compassion strengthens those neural pathways, which then makes practising self-compassion easier in the future.

SELF-ACCEPTANCE

The same goes for self-acceptance. Now, this is something that can take a long time to accomplish. However, I strongly believe that the younger we understand our need to take care of ourSELF, the less we will need to unpick later in life. We will already have the awareness and the tools. We will have developed a healthy habit of practising these things

naturally and regularly. I don't want you to wait until you're in your 30s or 40's when you first enter your personal development journey. Let's start now so you can enjoy life to the fullest and spend your 30s and 40's shining bright and living life your way.

Society is forever telling us that we need to or mustn't be this, that or the other. We're told that to be successful, we must get married, have kids, get a job in the city, make loads of money and be a version of ourselves that most people if they're honest, don't even like. People spend so much time trying to be something they're not that they end up a hot mess of stress and exhaustion.

Inner conflict is that feeling you get when you know something is off, but you can't quite put your finger on it. One part of you is saying one thing whilst the other part of you is contradicting that feeling and causing conflict within yourself. It goes back to your values not aligning with your current actions and behaviour. Accepting yourself will relieve that stress and reduce any inner conflict you may be having due to the mixed messages you keep receiving from all around you.

Let's face it; no one is ever going to match up to society's expectations. Accepting that we can't be all of the things all of the time is incredibly liberating. Accepting that some things are what they are, that some people will never change, and that you don't have to please everyone all of the time will free you from the stress and anxiety that non-acceptance brings.

Next time you're hard on yourself, ask yourself, "if a friend came to me being this hard on themselves, what would I say to them?" We are often very forgiving of others, but not ourselves, so start being kinder to yourself and showing yourself more compassion and acceptance. If anyone is going to be your biggest cheerleader, surely that person should be you.

Some signs that you're too hard on yourself are:

- You dwell on your mistakes and can't let go of them
- You're always comparing yourself to others
- You don't give your ideas the credit they deserve
- You spend a lot of time looking back at past mistakes
- You find it difficult to take a compliment without putting yourself down

SELF-LOVE AND FORGIVENESS

Forgive yourself and those around you. Holding onto your or your loved one's past mistakes is a sure way to keep yourself from acceptance. Let go of those mistakes and allow yourself to be okay with what happened. Forgiving others doesn't mean you have to allow them back in your life if you have distanced yourself. It just means you're not carrying around the emotions attached to them anymore.

Forgiveness is empowering, and it sets you free from emotional pain. If you're holding a grudge towards someone or someone has done wrong to you, it can become all-consuming in your mind and even cause physical illness. And it's the same when you're not forgiving yourself. When a grudge turns into long-term resentment, it can take over

your thought process and unbalance your emotional well-being. It stops you from living. You start to exist and focus on the wrongdoing instead of on your growth and positive experiences.

Think back to when someone did wrong and reflect on how you still carry that around. Then think about whether the other person is still carrying that around. Are they getting on with their life, their experiences whilst you're holding yourself back in the pain of it all? Is what happened still bothering them? The likelihood is that they are moving on with their lives whilst you're the one standing still. If you can learn to forgive and do it for yourself rather than the other person, you are back in control. If you can accept and let go of what happened, you can move on.

Now, I'm not suggesting that you don't feel anything. You will need to process the hurt, the anger, frustration and all the other emotions attached to what happened. But living in this state long-term allows them and what happened to hold all the control over your life. Letting go and forgiving will allow you to take back your power.

Here are two great exercises for letting go of your and other's past mistakes: The Letting Go Exercise and the Forgiveness exercise.

When something happens that knocks your confidence, you can all too often lose your self-esteem, and this is something that can take a long time to get back. Still, the good news is that you can rebuild your self-esteem and become a more confident version of yourself.

LETTING GO EXERCISE

Find a quiet space where you can sit for a few minutes without being disturbed.

1. Close your eyes and imagine your emotion (e.g. anger) as balloons that you are holding.

2. You can even give each balloon a specific feeling regarding your anger, e.g. frustration, aggression, confusion, and anger.

3. Imagine that each balloon holds one of these words inside and release all the balloons together.

4. Watch your anger, frustration or confusion float away.

5. Keep watching them until they disappear entirely from sight high up in the sky.

6. Open your eyes and notice the calmness that you now feel within yourself.

7. Write down anything you would do differently if you went back to that disagreement now that you have put yourself in the other person's shoes and seen it as an outsider.

8. Would you have dealt with things differently? What have you learnt that you could use the next time you find yourself in a similar situation?

FORGIVENESS MEDITATION

Forgiveness and sending love to people that have harmed you is more of a healing process for yourself.

1. Bring your attention to your heart and direct your breath there.

2. See an image of yourself deep within your heart.

3. See yourself happy and healthy.

4. Repeat the following to yourself in your head or out loud "May I enjoy happiness" for about 30 seconds.

5. Repeat the same process with someone you love "May (name) enjoy happiness."

6. Then again, with a friend.

7. Then again, with someone you're less fond of.

8. Then again, with someone who you feel has done you wrong.

9. Let your heart open and reach out to them, invite them within yourself, and wish them all the happiness you want for yourself and even more.

SELF-ESTEEM

Self-esteem is how you see yourself, your abilities and your limitations. When your self-esteem is healthy, you feel good about yourself and recognise you deserve all the good things. When you experience low self-esteem, you put little value on your opinions and ideas. You may decide that you're not good enough.

Your self-esteem starts to form in early childhood; those around you and your experiences at home and school will influence you. If you mainly receive positive feedback, you're more likely to see yourself as worthy and have healthy self-esteem. However, suppose you spend much time receiving criticism and have others tease you, you're more likely to experience lower self-esteem.

It may surprise you that the most significant factor on your self-esteem lives in your mind. Your thoughts have one of the greatest impacts on you, which are in your control; you can start to change those thoughts for ones that better support your self-worth.

If you're focusing on your weaknesses and telling yourself that you can't do new things or you're not good enough at something, you will impact your self-esteem. If you focus on your personal strengths and qualities, you can re-frame your thoughts about yourself and build your self-worth.

YOU ARE WORTHY!
YOU ARE ENOUGH!

It's natural for you to feel down on yourself at times. It's

part of life, but be mindful that this doesn't spiral into a way of life. When life gets you down, allow yourself some time to process what's happening. Then feel all the feelings and take some time to be kind and compassionate to yourself and re-focus on your values, strengths and qualities to help you re-balance yourself and get back on your feet.

Other things that can affect your sense of worth include the media. Comparing yourself to what you perceive as 'perfect' on social media can significantly affect how you see yourself. In this age of Instagram, Snap chat and TikTok, you are bombarded daily with airbrushed and filtered images. These can lead you to believe that this is the way you should look, what you should think, and how to live - and it's fake. If you're comparing yourself to this barrage of unrealistic, unachievable crap, then don't be surprised if you start to feel less yourself; less capable, less good enough, less clever enough etc. It damages your self-esteem if you cannot separate fact from fiction in this content.

Ask any Instagram influencer how many times she had to shoot that video to get the perfect lighting for her perfect tan. Or how long it took to capture that photo with the perfect hair curl or whiteness of her teeth or practice sitting uncomfortably in a particular pose to get it to what they perceive to be perfect. Have you tried any of these ridiculous poses? Such as falling off chairs into the swimming pool or off the window ledge whilst trying to recreate something once that took them weeks to get right, and it's still only right for a split second.

Yes, perfection is a perception. No one person perceives

perfect to mean the same thing. When you think of perfection, what does it mean to you? Your perfect may never match another person's perfect and vice versa, so looking for perfection is exhausting. It can lead to stress and anxiety due to the all-consuming nature of feeling like you have failed if you're not perfect or don't have a perfect life.

As a recovering perfectionist myself, it was so freeing when I realised all of this and started to be kinder to myself. I used to believe that I had to be the perfect child. I accepted that perfect is not real and that I'll never meet my family's idea of perfect. Why? Because when I was a kid, my parents would tell this same story repeatedly about the time we went to a restaurant after a day out. It was nearing closing time, and the waitress was hesitant as to whether to let us in or not. My parents said that she was worried that because we were young kids, we might be noisy, walk around or be a nuisance when all she wanted to do was shut shop and go home. My dad managed to convince her, and we sat down. I have no recollection of this event, but I've heard this story so many times that I believe the way it's been told to me to be true. However, the perception of the event is tinted by my parent's beliefs on how children should behave.

We had our food, and apparently, the waitress came over and said she was wrong to be hesitant. My sister and I had been very well behaved and complimented my parents on how good we had been. So from a young age, I began to think that to be accepted and allowed to do anything, I had to be perfect. I had to be quiet and still and be a good girl.

I come from a background where I would so often hear

the expression 'children should be seen and not heard!' And wow, did this give me some confidence and self-esteem issues around being louder, being listened to and being deserving of being able to use my voice to express myself.

As young children, we take on so much of what people say to us that we begin to believe that that's who we are and what we deserve. Being told that you don't deserve something because you haven't been good enough is something else that can hold you back as you get older. You may start to believe that you're not deserving, but you are. Remember, though, that I take into account with my parents that they too were parented in the same way, so the cycle continued. It was up to me to break that cycle when I had my children. It is the same for many families.

We spoke about parental cycles earlier in the book, which are further examples of the impact they can have on you growing up. Now you're a teenager, you can start becoming aware of which ones you want to take forward in life and which you want to leave behind to build your self-esteem and confidence.

If you ever feel that you may be spiralling and unable to re-balance yourself, speak to a trusted adult who can support you to do this. Talking about feelings and challenges has a powerful impact. You may have heard the saying 'a problem shared is a problem halved.' And it's so true. Speaking about things makes us feel better; we feel seen, heard, and understood. If you find it hard to talk to your parents or carer, you can speak to a trusted teacher, pastoral support in school, a classroom support worker, or a school counsellor if available.

If you find it difficult to open up to people you know, then there are phone support and text support helplines that you can contact. YoungMinds is one I always recommend, as you can use their text service to speak to someone who can offer you some initial support. You can find their details on the resources page.

With well-balanced self-esteem, you can express your needs and opinions, make decisions confidently, and deal with daily stresses in a healthy, well-balanced way. You are able to create healthy relationships, not be over-critical, and have a realistic view of yourself and your capabilities.

Your self-esteem can fluctuate throughout life depending on what you're dealing with at any given time. But if you can remember to feel, process and re-focus when you're feeling less than confident about life, then you'll be in a good position to recognise and boost your self-esteem over time. Remember, none of what you're learning in this book is an overnight magic pill. You're on a growth journey, and life has its ups and downs. However, after reading this book, you will feel better equipped to deal with those ups and downs and feel more confident about being yourself and living the best and most balanced version of YOU. The thought of that gives me immense joy, and I'm incredibly grateful that you have chosen to take this journey with my support.

YOU ARE ENOUGH WITHOUT ALL THE STUFF!

Can we talk about material items for a minute while talking about your self-worth, please?

In this age of instant gratification, where you can order stuff and have it quickly, society relies on having 'stuff' to fill

the gap where other, more important things belong, like joy, gratitude and happiness. Pleasure is taking over, and people are mistaking pleasure for happiness. You see, pleasure is generally instant, yet happiness is long-term. Nobody wants to wait for anything anymore, so they'll settle for pleasure rather than create true happiness for themselves.

An example is ordering things off Amazon that you don't need or want. Trust me; you can convince yourself that you need or want these things. You can tell yourself all the stories you need to, but if you take a step back, ask yourself if you really need or want them or if you are looking for something to make you feel good at that moment and fulfil that need for pleasure.

Take a moment now to think about what happiness means to you. When you hear the word happiness, what comes to mind? We all have different ideas of what happiness means to us, just like success. It means different things to different people. Some people see happiness as having a lovely house, living in a specific town, or by the seaside. Some people see it as having a family and being able to spend time with them. Others consider success to be making lots of money, whilst others see it as getting married and having kids. Working out your concept of happiness and success will support you to live a life that gives you your version of each of these.

CHAPTER TEN

ANXIETY

Everyone experiences anxiety and worry sometimes. Like any other emotion, it's important to recognise when and what's happening and how often. It's your body's warning system. It lets you know that something needs your attention and that we need to take action on something.

Why does anxiety have its very own chapter if it's an emotion?

Since Covid, we as a society are seeing a considerable increase in the number of young people experiencing it, particularly around school and socialising. So I want to ensure that you have a greater understanding of what it is, why it happens and how you can support yourself, a friend, or a family member.

The first thing is to understand that a bit of anxiety is a good thing. It keeps you alert, helps you avoid dangerous situations, and motivates you to deal with problems as they arise. It's only when anxiety takes over and becomes a way of life that we need to pay closer attention.

A healthy amount of nerves and worry is like a healthy habit as it becomes automatic. You feel it; you know it's there, but you can move past it pretty quickly and do what you need to do. However, when it becomes unhealthy, it's with you most of the time in most situations. It's time to take

notice and speak to a trusted friend or adult to find extra support.

I best describe anxiety as your mind living in the future and negatively using your imagination to create a danger that isn't real. Humans like to predict the future or mind read to feel safer. This can get out of control when you're sitting in your emotional mind; this is where you need to find the rational mind to re-balance yourself. You can do this using the Reality exercise in chapter 8.

So how do you know if anxiety is what you're experiencing?

There are a whole host of symptoms when experiencing this emotion. With increased self-awareness, you can recognise these symptoms quite quickly and use breathing techniques to bring yourself out of your mind and back into your body to ground yourself.

Anxiety symptoms come from the feeling of threat. Historically, there was the threat of physical danger from a wild animal or of the enemy hunting us. As a result, our bodies have developed a specific response to those fears, which we now call the 'fight, flight or freeze' response. They're quite easy to remember as fight speaks for itself. You start to lash out, get agitated and may even punch walls or physically hurt someone. Flight means to run away from it; you avoid it. For example, if you're worried about school work that you don't understand or having a problem with a friend, you may try to avoid them. Freeze means that you do nothing, you remain stuck, or your body literally freezes like a statue at that moment.

You may experience a dry mouth, sweaty hands, increased heart rate and shortness of breath. You may feel like you might faint and feel your body heat rising from your toes to your head. Although not in physical danger, your body still reacts in this same way to protect you from harm. Let's take a chameleon, for example. When they feel in danger and believe a predator is nearby, they freeze, as do many animals. They do this in the hope that their enemy won't see them, so initially, they turn their freeze response on, then they might switch response and enter the flight response where they'll run as fast as they can to find a safe place. You can use two or even all of these when your mind alerts you to a perceived danger.

Interestingly when it comes to other people and your need for community, your survival response is heightened. Your survival instinct believes that you need to be accepted by others to fit in or feel good enough. Disapproval from other group members can flick the switch on those responses as it's so deeply embedded in us as humans to be part of a pack. Like lions, tigers and wild dogs, we are pack animals. It is why community and connection are so important to us; when your mind feels that you're being left out or disapproved of by friends and family, your response pattern will ignite.

Your anxiety might be triggered when you remember an event or imagine an event where you didn't 'fit in.' The memory can send you into an anxiety spiral where you may feel any or all of these things; isolated, sick, butterflies in your tummy, hot flushes, loss of appetite, numbness, dizziness, confusion, an inability to remember things and headaches.

You may feel your body physically wanting to run away but also feeling frozen to the spot. Try to allow this feeling to flow through you as it won't last forever. Like all emotions, if you allow it to wash over you, you are more likely to re-balance and find your calm more easily.

Although anxiety is most commonly linked to the future, there are two other key sources: the past and the present. If we experience worry about the past, it's because we are worried that an event or experience may happen again. Your mind can become ultra-sensitive to anything that may slightly resemble what happened and will hijack your thoughts around a situation. When this occurs, it sends you back into your fight, flight or freeze response, pushing any rational thoughts to the back of your mind until the experience happens again in your mind. You act through your emotional mind and create something that isn't necessarily real and hasn't even happened yet.

Anxiety can also directly result from something happening in the here and now. You can become fearful through your perception of imminent danger. In the moment, anxiety is more often than not beneficial to us as it's telling us we need to act. This can support us in making a decision, taking action or resolving a problem.

For each of these anxiety sources, the following exercises are great for bringing you back into balance. Once you've found your balance, the Reality exercise is a great one to use so you can work out if there really is a threat or if your emotional mind is hijacking you and pushing your rational mind out of the way.

7-11 BREATHING

You can find one quick and helpful tool when we feel our stress and anxiety rise: 'the breath.' Knowing how to breathe through the feeling is a great tool to have in your toolbox for yourself or when you witness someone else feeling stressed and anxious.

In general, we don't breathe correctly. We don't breathe slowly or deep enough to give effective oxygen levels. Consciously slowing our breath down will allow more oxygen into our brains and body enabling us to bring ourselves down from feeling out of control.

Make a note of this simple yet hugely effective tool. Practice it regularly until it becomes natural to tune into the breath when you can feel yourself or notice your tween or teen escalating into a state of nervousness or panic.

- Breathe in slowly and fully into your diaphragm, watching your belly go in and out
- Count to seven as you breathe in
- Then count to eleven as you breathe out
- Keep this up for a few minutes or for as long as you need
- Notice the anxious feeling subside

GROUNDING EXERCISE

If you find yourself or a family member struggling with negative thoughts or feelings, it can help to ground yourself by focusing on the things around you at that moment.

This is such a simple and effective technique.

- Name five things you can see
- Name four things you can touch or feel
- Name three things you can hear
- Name two things you can smell
- Name one thing you can taste

When you've gone through this list, your nervous system and your breathing will start to regulate, and you'll feel much calmer.

Working with young people, I come across anxiety pretty much every day. I, of course, experience it myself, as do the people I love. Your world experience is unique, so don't think you can't overcome your anxiety if the first technique doesn't work for you. Not every method works for everyone, so try out a few and see which ones suit your needs.

Take a young girl who came to me for help as she avoided college work. She fell behind due to a lack of confidence in her abilities. As a result, she started to worry that she would fail, that her classmates and her tutor would reject her, and that she would be called useless. This thought was backing up the belief she had around herself, so to think this made it a fact in her mind. The secondary school provided the girl with learning support for the first two years. After that, she could not access the necessary support, which enabled her to back up her belief that she was a failure, she wasn't good enough and wasn't accepted. As a result, her emotional mind took over, and she continued to tell herself that she couldn't do it.

She entered a flight response, and she avoided college for weeks. She would come in now and then, but then she became overwhelmed with what she needed to do, further avoiding her learning. This continued for over six months until we sat down and spoke about how she felt and what support she needed. Once we met those needs, she was on her way, and six weeks later, she walked out of college with her full qualification. She was proud of herself and with more confidence and belief in her abilities and techniques that she could use throughout life whenever things seemed scary and overwhelming.

Asking for help is not a weakness! You can do anything, but you can't do everything! We all need help and support at times.

Whilst studying, I discovered the fantastic teachings of Joe Griffin and Ivan Tyrell. They created the Human Givens approach in the late 90s based on a practical, holistic and scientific approach focussing on what individuals need to live physically and emotionally healthy lives.

It's here that I learned in depth about our physical and emotional human needs, and I use these as a framework for my practice with young people. I also host family needs audits to create more harmony in the home. When a family's needs are being met in the home, it makes a calmer place for everyone to live and reduces stress and anxiety in both the individuals and family unit.

When one or more of your needs is not being met in balance, it can cause stress and anxiety, which is why I include these needs within this chapter. See if any of these needs are unmet for you, which are in balance, and which are being met, but perhaps not healthily. The aim is to get your needs met healthily and in balance while helping those around you meet theirs.

You can find more information on this at **www.humangivens.com**

PHYSICAL AND EMOTIONAL NEEDS

Food and drink - These are our most basic needs, ones we take for granted if we are fortunate, but even these basic needs are not always met in a given moment. Have you ever heard the expression 'Hangry?' It's when you're hungry and making you angry, short-tempered and agitated. You may think it's because of something else when you're just hungry and need to refuel. You can forget this need when doing homework or out with friends until the hanger mood kicks in. Likewise, most people don't drink enough during the day, which can cause confusion, lack of motivation, headaches and a lack of focus.

Sleep - You must have heard a family member ask you if you're tired - the first sign of irritability, and we all blame it on being tired. Although it's not always the answer, a lack of quality sleep can have a range of effects on you both physically and emotionally. Have you ever noticed that you are more emotional when you've not had a good sleep? You can be short-tempered and lack patience with yourself and others. Getting a good night's sleep as regularly as possible is essential. This means not staying up late staring at your phone or watching Netflix!

Movement - Are you moving enough daily? I'm not talking about it having to be a big sports game or hours of exercise. I'm referring to getting your body moving and being mindful of how often you're being active in one way or another. Taking a walk, a bike ride, swimming or other activity. Movement is essential for both physical and emotional well-being and is a great way to overcome some of the stresses and worries of life.

Security - This one is about safety. Do you feel safe in your environment? Is there anywhere you don't feel safe,

and have you told a trusted adult if that is the case? This is one of your number one needs. You feel safe when your caregiver holds you as a child and if someone picks you up when you're crying and scared. As you get older, this need remains but is met differently. A hug is the equivalent of being picked up when scared, and an arm around your shoulder can replace being held when upset. Do you feel secure, either with others or alone? If this need is unmet, it can lead to stress and anxiety. Your need for security can be different from a friend or family member.

Attention - Do you feel you get enough attention? Are you perhaps receiving too much attention? Are you giving attention as well as receiving it? Some people need more attention than others, and it's good to recognise those friends and family members to whom this applies so you can better understand their needs and your own. Children generally need more attention and will do anything to get it, even if that means acting out. This can lead to a pattern of repeat behaviour if they get used to their needs being met by acting out. This need is not being met in a healthy way when this happens, and they may find they're getting more and more negative attention from parents, teachers, friends, etc. It feels good to give others attention; if you want attention, you need to give it.

Emotional Connection - Do you feel emotionally connected to others? Everyone needs at least one person in their life that they feel accepts them fully for who they are. Do you have a person like this? You can also meet the need through having fun with friends and being close with a partner. When this need is unmet, you might feel lonely.

Emotional connection to yourself is as important as your connection to others. You can build a connection with others through sharing time and creating ideas with friends and peers at school. Get involved in group activities with people who share your passions and interests. Is someone you know too heavily reliant on you for their emotional connection? This can be draining and create stress within yourself, so be mindful if this is happening.

Control/Autonomy - Everyone you meet feels like they need to have some control over their lives and be allowed the freedom to make their own choices. Never being allowed to make your own decisions can feel unfair and can be a source of stress, leading to anxiety. When a person doesn't feel like they are in control of things in life, e.g. work or school, they may seek more control in another area, such as at home. Where is your need for autonomy not being met, and how are you seeking it elsewhere? It's important to get this need met in balance as too much control can also create stress and anxiety. The need for everything to be perfect can be exhausting. Remember you cannot control other people, and trying to do so will result in emotional exhaustion for both parties. How can you get this need met in a healthy and balanced way?

Sense of Achievement - Do you know the things that you are good at? Recognising what you're good at can boost your sense of achievement which feels good. It doesn't matter how big or small you think the achievement is, acknowledge it and celebrate it. Everyone needs to know that they matter and have skills they can grow and use that others may not have. You can meet this need by setting

goals and challenges to find the things you're good at and how to improve them or learn something new.

Respect - Your need for respect is likely to differ from those you spend time with. It's important to feel like a valued family member and appreciated by your friends or respected for your opinions and ideas. Your status within your friendship group is also included in this need for respect. However, having an over-inflated sense of the status of yourself is not healthily meeting this need. Remember that respect is earned and not given; it's a two-way street, so if you want respect, show respect! Is this need being met healthily? Are you showing respect as well as receiving it?

Privacy - As you enter your teenage years, your need for privacy, alongside autonomy, increases. When you were younger, you relied heavily on your caregivers for these things. As you mature, you want more control over these things, which, if you have younger siblings, can prove difficult when they burst into your room every five minutes. Sometimes you need to be alone to reflect and gain perspective on a situation or talk to your friends. When this need isn't met, you may look for privacy more and exclude yourself from those around you. You may avoid being with others and feel overloaded when in other people's company for too long, so balancing this need is important. Some people have a greater need for privacy than others. Recognising when you isolate yourself to meet this need is a sign that this needs your attention.

Community - As a human being, you're naturally a pack animal, so your need for community is important. Feeling part of a group can boost this need and your need for respect and achievement. If this need is unmet, you can start feeling isolated and lonely, leading to stress and anxiety. How are you meeting this need at the moment? Are you part of a group? Are you mixing with your community?

Meaning and Purpose - You may have been asked what you want to be when you leave school, and this is all part of starting your journey to discovering your purpose in life. Your need for meaning and purpose is often about something more significant and outside of yourself that you're passionate about. Something that lights you up and is your reason for getting out of bed. The need to stretch out of your comfort zone and believe in something bigger than the everyday. You can begin to feel stressed when this need is unmet as it can lead to feelings of frustration and helplessness, which feeds into the need for achievement.

When you start to feel anxious or stressed, refer back to your needs and see which one or ones aren't being met at that moment. Make a note of each of these needs and do a regular audit with yourself to see which ones need rebalancing.

Practice this often, and in time you will see straight away where things have become out of balance and how to rebalance them. You will also start to recognise where your friends and family's needs are out of balance and will be able to support them in rebalancing theirs too.

To sign off this chapter, I want you to remember to breathe...yes it sounds so simple. When you know how to do

it effectively, it is, but life is hectic. When you're constantly on the go, you're not breathing fully, so the maximum amount of oxygen needed isn't entering the body. Breathing in and out fully when you feel stress or anxiety rising is incredibly effective. Focusing on the breath will bring you out of your mind and back into your body. At that moment, you want to stop thinking and start feeling the emotions pass through you.

CHAPTER ELEVEN

WAYS TO IMPROVE YOUR WELL-BEING

In this chapter, I want to focus on giving you a valuable toolkit I wish I'd had in my teenage years. If I had been able to quieten the negative voices in my mind from an earlier age, it would have made my late teens and early 20's an entirely different experience. I contemplated taking my own life when I was nineteen after my split with my first serious boyfriend. Working with young girls struggling with self-worth, I know these tools will also make a difference for you.

MINDFULNESS

Mindfulness isn't all about sitting crossed-legged in meditation with your hands on your knees and making funny noises. I used to think it was, but having been introduced to it during my coaching and practitioner training, I soon realised that mindfulness is about being in the moment in everyday situations. It's about being still, clearing your mind and allowing your thoughts and feelings to flow through you.

Mindfulness is about finding inner calm and taking notice by using all of your senses to focus more on what's happening to you and around you. It supports you to increase your self-esteem, build self-confidence and create self-acceptance.

For example, when you're in your room watching your favourite film or Netflix series, playing on the PlayStation or

scrolling TikTok, you're entirely focused. You almost step into the screen as all your senses are on high alert, so it feels like the sights, sounds, smells, and feelings surrounding you are happening rather than just on the screen. You're so focused and submerged in it that you can't hear your mum shouting for the third time that dinner is ready or her asking you to come and lay the table or empty the dishwasher.

Mindfulness is just like that but for real life. By focusing on the current moment as it's happening, rather than automatically thinking about what's next, around the corner or what happened yesterday, allows you to appreciate what's happening now and reflect on what's going on for you. Mindfulness is a skill; the good news is you can learn it. One person's mindful space is not necessarily another person's calm place. Finding your calm space where you feel you can be mindful will help you start this journey. It will enable you to come back here for self-reflection, perhaps at the end or beginning of each day. You may discover that walking in nature, running, sitting in the park or having a bath is where you are most mindful. I can assure you that your phone is not the place. Scrolling through social media overstimulates your brain and heightens your stress hormones. I'm sure you've noticed that you can feel agitated when you come off social media. A parent or sibling may have mentioned that you're rude or abrupt when they speak to you and you're 'in the scroll.' Your brain is trying to keep up with all the immediate content, and your senses are overloaded. By all means, use your phone for music and perhaps download the Calm app or something similar, which you can use when in your mindful space.

As with all things, mindfulness takes practice. But I promise you once you're in the habit, it will become as natural to you as cleaning your teeth or tying your shoelaces. The difference it will make to you will be recognised by yourself and those around you.

Here are some well-being and mindfulness techniques to get you started.

GROUNDING

As mentioned in Chapter 10. If you find yourself or a member of your family struggling with negative thoughts or feelings, it can help to ground yourself by focusing on the things around you at that moment.

This is such a simple and effective technique.

- Name five things you can see
- Name four things you can touch or feel
- Name three things you can hear
- Name two things you can smell
- Name one thing you can taste

When you've gone through the list, your nervous system and your breathing will start to regulate, and you'll feel much calmer.

ANCHORING

You can use your senses to unlock memories and feelings. As a result, you can create anchors for yourself to boost confidence, create calm or stimulate your happy hormones.

It is an anchor if you have a song that makes you think

about a person or special occasion, such as Christmas or being with a friend. The song's familiarity triggers your happy hormones, and you instantly feel that emotion rise in your body, making you smile and think of that occasion. The same can be said for a special toy you had when you were a young child. Or a specific smell, like your nan's perfume; whenever you smell it anywhere, you think of her straight away, and the memories you have with her flood your mind.

Even better than this is that you can create a new anchor for whatever feeling you want to have more of, and this is incredibly powerful stuff. You can find yourself a smooth stone, a song you like or a particular sound like a bell. Or even a taste or simply an action like clenching your first firmly when you want to feel confident about something. I also use this one and have anchored it for my two girls. When we doubt ourselves or need a little boost when we're about to do something difficult, we clench our first tight, so we can feel its strength and tell ourselves, 'I've got this,' and off we go. It sounds too simple to be true, but it works - give it a go.

So how do we anchor the feeling to the object, song, person, taste etc.?

Sit somewhere quiet where you won't be disturbed and think of the last time you felt your happiest, calmest, most confident (whatever the feeling is you want to recreate). Whilst doing this, rub your fingers over the stone, taste the taste, listen to the song or put on the perfume. Do this a few times over and over. You may need to return to this a few times to set a strong anchor. The next time you feel down, you need a confidence boost, or to feel calmer, go back to your anchor and the feeling you attached to it. Think of how you feel when 'I wish you a Merry Christmas' comes on the radio every year. Your anchor will fill your mind and body just as when you set it.

You can even use this technique for exams, public speaking, walking into a classroom, and meeting new people. You can even create different anchors for different needs. For example, you could use the stone for anything happening at school as no one will know you have it, and a song at home that you can put on whenever you need it. Your anchor can be so subtle that only you know it's even there.

MEDITATION

This is something that I wish I'd known about when I was a teenager. It's something that I have introduced my girls to, and I'm pleased to say that they have taken to it and already see the benefits.

You can meditate in many ways, and you can find great examples on YouTube or using an app such as Headspace or Calm.

You can meditate on absolutely anything. You can be intentional or allow the thoughts to flow like clouds in the sky and reflect on what comes up at that moment. I always recommend using a guided meditation when you first begin and start small, so start with a couple of minutes and build up from there. You don't need to be meditating for an hour at a time. Topping up for 5-10 minutes daily is enough to impact your self-awareness and reflection significantly.

The very first meditation I would suggest is where you first close your eyes and take a couple of deep breaths in and out. On returning your breath to a regular breathing pattern, allow yourself to notice the thoughts that come into your mind, recognise them and watch them float by whilst seeing where the emotions attached to these thoughts sit in your body. Do this for about five minutes and note down the thoughts and feelings that stuck out to you and where they appeared in your body.

The second one I always suggest, once you've done the first daily for a week, is to do the same thing. However, this time instead of allowing the thoughts to flow, try to clear your mind and let yourself be still physically and emotionally and see if you can push the thoughts away if they come into your mind. They will try to make their way in. When they do this, thank the thought, let it know that you don't need it now, and watch it leave. This one takes more practice, so keep this up each day for a couple of weeks. Some people never manage to master this particular meditation, and that's okay. If it doesn't work for you, go back to the first one, or try a focused meditation like the ones in the following examples.

Before you begin, ensure that you're in a quiet space that allows you to relax and where you won't be disturbed for the duration of your meditation. There are no rules, but I recommend you find a regular time in the day. I find bedtime a good time as it has an even more powerful impact on the next day, but some people like to do it in the morning to set them up for the day.

Once your meditation practice is over, you may find it

helpful to write what came up during meditation. It's a great way to check in with yourself. You have more clarity to find solutions to a problem you may be having, some of which you may not even have been consciously aware of but have come up in meditation.

Meditation is an excellent self-awareness tool; once mastered, you can tap into this state whenever and wherever.

Here are a few examples of things you can meditate on:

- A problem that you've been struggling to resolve
- A big decision that you need to make
- An achievement you have had recently
- Reflection on what's happened today
- Setting the intention on how you want tomorrow to go
- How you want to feel about something or someone

As with everything, practice makes progress (not perfect!). Be kind to yourself, and don't be hard on yourself if this takes you a while to get used to. It took me some time as quietening my mind proved difficult for a while, but I'm so glad I persevered with it. It's my go-to when I need to find inner peace or calm my mind from the day's chaos.

SLEEP

I love to sleep! I'm a proper snuggle under the covers 7-8 hours a night kind of girl, and to be honest, I always have been. Without sleep, I am not the most pleasant person to be around. I need more sleep than a lot of people I know. As a teenager, I must have slept more than the average person my age.

With all the development and changes going on in your

body, you probably notice that you, too, are sleeping longer and having a nap in the afternoon. Your body clock might be all over the place due to napping and lying in until late morning, or early afternoon, especially on the weekends.

Whilst you sleep, your body is repairing, resting and getting ready for the next day. If you're not getting enough quality sleep, your body cannot fully repair and prepare. It can lead to feeling tired, irritable, stressed and unwell if it goes on for a while. You may dream, which can sometimes result from your brain processing what happened that day.

Feeling tired can make you grumpy and more prone to big emotions. You may act more dramatically than usual or be mean to people without fully understanding what's happening. Becoming mindful of when you have not had enough sleep is key to identifying the behaviour resulting from that. You can then take a step back and do something about it.

Children between the ages of five and twelve should get roughly 9-12 hours of sleep. Pre-teens and teenagers up to eighteen between 8-10 hours a night and age eighteen plus 6-8 hours. Are you getting enough sleep?

If you find getting to sleep difficult, don't worry, you're not alone. I speak to people who find it hard to calm their minds for long enough to fall asleep. They lay awake thinking about everything they didn't get done, didn't say, didn't have, and worry about tomorrow.

If this is you, then fear not, as I have the perfect mindfulness exercise for you to try, the Body scan technique for sleep.

BODY SCAN TECHNIQUE FOR SLEEP

This tool is particularly effective when you're having trouble switching off your mind for sleep. It can also be used in times of stress and when feeling anxious. In a nutshell, you talk to your body to relax and distract your mind from all the thoughts keeping you awake.

In your head, tell each part of your body to relax. Do this using a slow and gentle inner voice. Start with your toes and tell them to relax, completely and totally relax. Move on to your whole foot, and tell it to relax, completely and totally relax. Then move on to your ankle, lower leg, knees etc., until you reach your head, where you will also tell each part of your face to relax. Finish by telling your whole body to relax completely and totally, and then start from your toes again if needed.

I guarantee you're unlikely to get this far; nine times out of ten, you will be ready to drift off before this point. It's my favourite technique for sleep that I've been using for myself, my family, and clients with great success.

Creating a healthy bedtime routine will also aid you in more restful sleep. This may be reading a book or listening to calming music. Or try writing your thoughts in a journal, get organised for the next day, or take a nice warm bath or shower. Give some of these a go and see which works for you. Do not use screens for at least thirty minutes before bedtime. This stimulates your brain activity and reverses what's needed to drift off to sleep.

GRATITUDE

The next time you feel a little jealous or compare yourself to someone at school who has the latest trainers, a friend who's going on holiday abroad or someone on social media who has more followers than you, turn your focus to gratitude. Jealousy will only breed more jealousy. It will become a habit, and you will see even more things to be jealous about in your everyday life.

Humans are hard-wired to see threats, so it's no wonder that you automatically seek and notice negative emotions such as jealousy. If you switch your focus to what you have to be grateful for daily, you will begin to see more things to be thankful for. You'll form a new, healthier habit that will have you feeling lighter, brighter and happier in your new-found positive, grateful way of life.

Focusing on what you do have rather than what you don't have brings happiness through becoming mindful of your positive traits, strengths and uniqueness. Perhaps instead of focusing on your friend going on holiday, you could focus on what you can do in that time that will make you happy. Maybe try something new, go somewhere you've not been in ages or spend time with someone you've not seen for some time. Sometimes when you are jealous, it's not because of what the other person is doing; it's because you're not doing what deep down you know you could be doing to make yourself happier. Use this as a kick up the arse to do it, and then note how grateful you have been to do it.

Things to be grateful for include how strong your body is and how it supports you. Your breath because without it, you wouldn't be alive. Use it wisely. More on that later! I'm sure you're probably taking your family and friends and how they have your back when you need them for granted; we all do it. YOURSELF, don't forget to be grateful for who you are and what you offer the world.

Notice the big and the little things every day, and start your new attitude of gratitude by noting down three things you're grateful for each day. Such as the sun shining when you've got to walk to school or college. The rain falls when it's too hot to get on the bus. Your favourite song was playing on the radio. Start with the small things. It may be difficult at first as your mind will automatically wander to the negative things that happened, like being caught at every set of traffic lights on the bus, getting wet in the rain, or you did something wrong today, and you're hard on yourself as a result.

Let those negative thoughts pass through your mind like clouds pass through the sky. Try using the grounding technique before you do this, as it will help to clear your mind of all the negative chatter so you can tune into the positives.

Attach this new gratitude habit to another habit you already have embedded in your mind, like cleaning your teeth at night or washing your face. That way, it will become part of your routine quicker.

LEAD WITH LOVE AND KINDNESS

Your body responds to love and kindness in the same way that it responds to stress and anger. It's all about where you focus your mind.

You can get caught up in the negative spiral of your thoughts and feelings. When you're feeling all those big emotions and living through your emotional mind, it can be hard to pick out the love and kindness around you. When you fall out with your family or friends, it can feel like the world is against you, which can make you feel isolated from others and your own reality.

When was the last time you showed yourself or another person love and kindness? How can you show more love and kindness to yourself and others?

I see so many young girls who are down on themselves, who spend so much time focusing on their weaknesses, faults and flaws that they completely wipe out any form of love and kindness towards themselves. They then project these feelings onto their friends and family. Then it becomes a vicious circle that gets bigger and bigger until it's so big that it causes stress, isolation and sometimes even self-harm to deal with the emotional pain of being out of control or feeling the need to FEEL something due to the numbness that now consumes them.

If you or anyone you know is thinking about or talking about self-harming, it's time to reach out to a trusted adult to provide the proper support. You can refer to the self-harm chapter for more information on this.

Practising love and kindness will bring you back to reality, re-balance your emotional and rational mind, and flood your body with warmth. It's a great way to grow a social connection and is good for your overall health and well-being.

We can do this using the Love and Kindness exercise. You may find it challenging at first, and you may want to take this slowly as it can bring up some strong emotions. If it does, remind yourself that you are safe and allow the emotion to flow through you being mindful of where you feel it and the thoughts coming up. If you need to stop at any time, do so and come back to it when you're ready.

Suppose you have fallen out with a friend. In that case, you can send them kindness and to yourself, giving you physical and emotional relief from the situation. Remember that you are safe if you start to feel big emotions rising. If it's too much, stop and come back to it another time. It may be too soon after the event, and your emotions may be too raw.

It's always a good idea to write down how this felt and recognise the thoughts and emotions attached.

RANDOM ACTS OF KINDNESS

Random acts of kindness are also a great way for us to support other people to feel good whilst making ourselves feel good too. When someone pays you a compliment, it feels good,

LOVE AND KINDNESS EXERCISE

Get into a comfortable position

- Close your eyes and take 2 or 3 deep breaths before returning to your usual breathing pattern
- Relax your body
- When you're ready, bring to mind a person you care about and someone who, when they're happy, makes you happy
- When you have that person in your mind, silently say to them, "may you be happy". "May you be well."
- You're sending them a friendly wish for happiness and health
- Repeat three times and feel how it feels in your body
- Then switch your focus to yourself. You deserve kindness too
- Silently say, "may I be happy." "May I be well." "May I not be overwhelmed with stress."

When you are comfortable doing this exercise, you can start to bring in other people and gradually offer kindness to those around you and even people you don't necessarily know. You can also send love and kindness to someone you feel may have done wrong to you as part of forgiveness, ensuring you show yourself kindness at the same time.

doesn't it, and when you pay others a compliment, it feels good too. A simple smile floods your body with happy hormones, and the same feeling occurs when someone smiles at you.

One thing I tell my clients is that when someone pays you a compliment, don't dismiss it or turn it into a negative. Simply say thank you. If you dismiss it, you make the other person feel bad or awkward, and you're also telling yourself that you don't deserve to be complimented, and YOU DO! Next time someone compliments you on something, be aware of your response and stop yourself from putting yourself down. Practise on a friend tomorrow and see what happens. Or get a friend or family member to pay you a compliment so you can practise saying thank you and stopping yourself from following that up with 'it's too short' or 'no, I don't' or 'I look stupid' or 'are you taking the mickey?' The more you can take a compliment, the easier it will become and the more comfortable you will feel giving compliments to others too.

You can also show random acts of kindness by helping someone with their shopping bags, opening a door for someone or picking up something they have dropped. You might help an older person cross the road or give up your seat on the bus for a mum and her baby. All these little acts of kindness add up. They allow you to see the world through a more positive lens, and you'll start to notice when a stranger shows you kindness in the same way.

As a teenager, I saw all these things as a form of weakness. Why would I want to give up my seat? Why should I let someone on the bus before me? I get it; you don't deserve to treat yourself like a second-class citizen. My mistake was not

showing myself enough love and kindness simultaneously, so obviously, it felt like one-way traffic to me. It was like I was putting myself out and getting nothing back.

If I could go back, I would do things a little differently. I would be kinder to those around me whilst being kinder to myself. Showing myself more compassion and kindness would have changed so much for me. Leaving it until I was in my 40s was a big mistake and one I want to save you from having to make.

Everything in this book is geared toward supporting you to show yourself and others more love, compassion and understanding whilst boosting your confidence, self-esteem and belief that you are good enough - NO MATTER WHAT!

GETTING MORE ACTIVE

As young children, we tend to find being active very easy. Running, jumping, cycling, dancing and generally playing were all ways you were naturally active every day. You even learnt through play. You may have found that you have become less active in your teenage years.

As you mature, the sports you were once interested in no longer inspire or motivate you. You may find it harder to get out of bed and get yourself moving. You spend more time on your phone lounging around, and your energy levels feel much lower.

A personal trainer of mine once said, 'You need to use energy to gain energy.' She was so right. I hadn't even thought about it that way before, but I even remind myself of this when I'm not being active enough. Having been a gymnast for over ten years, training 15-20 hours a week, I had pretty much stopped exercising when I gave it up altogether at the age of seventeen. I lost all love for it. I had succumbed to being told I wasn't good enough and so decided there was no longer any point carrying on. As a result, I gave up on all physical activity for years after.

I had a client who was picked to run for her school and county on many occasions. She was an experienced runner but decided to give it all up at fifteen. She knew she was good at it, but as she grew and developed, it no longer fitted in with who she wanted to be and where she wanted to go. She discovered a completely new passion for painting. She spent all her time at the table with her paints and canvas, which was good for her well-being. She found it calming and helped her clear her mind after a difficult day.

Her parents were keen for her to go back to running, but the more they talked to her about it, the more she dug her heels in. When I asked her what running was giving her, she told me that it no longer gave her the same feeling it once had. She had become bored of its repetition and said that she had initially taken it up because it's what her mum had wanted her to do. Once she realised she was good at it, it gave her more confidence and a purpose as it was the only thing she felt good at.

As time passed by, she lost more and more interest and became less and less motivated until it came to a point where running made her feel worse about herself. She was forcing something that was no longer her, and she became disheartened by exercise altogether. It started to fill her with

dread, and she turned to paint more and more to help with these feelings.

We worked through those feelings, and she re-framed her thoughts and feelings around exercise. We devised some alternative ways for her to get more active around things she enjoyed. She now goes for a walk and finds inspiration for her paintings on those walks. She swims and even goes for a light jog. She does all of these things for the sake of enjoyment. We discovered that exercise had lost its sense of fun for her. The competition had got too much. It wasn't the running she now disliked; it was the seriousness that came with it. She needed to bring some fun back into it and know that she was doing it for enjoyment and her physical and emotional well-being.

You don't have to be doing something competitive to be active. You can move for fun. You can still run, jump, dance, play football or netball, or ride your bike purely to enjoy how it makes you feel and release those all-important happy hormones. When you feel good physically, you feel good emotionally too.

You don't need to be exercising for hours on end to feel the benefits. There are many ways that you can incorporate it into your day, and here are a few ideas for you:

- Go for a walk - take the dog or ask a friend to join you
- Try a 10-minute workout (you can find a lot on YouTube)
- Get off the bus one stop earlier and walk the rest of the way

- Take the stairs instead of the lift
- Do some cleaning and hoovering (your mum with love this one)
- Run around the block
- Go for a bike ride
- Learn Yoga

It's recommended that you do at least 30 minutes of activity a day. How are you going to be more active?

It's important to mention that your diet is important to your overall health and well-being, so be mindful of what you eat. It's all too easy to sit in your room on your phone snacking on crisps, chocolate, pastries, bacon sandwiches and other similar stuff. Think back to your NEEDS. Is your diet in balance?

CREATING A JOURNAL

Writing a diary might sound old-fashioned and not something that interests you, which is fair enough, but a journal is different. It's a place to reflect on your thoughts, feelings and behaviours of the day or week. There are no specific rules on how to use one, but here are some prompts that may be useful to help get you started.

You can write about:

- A happy memory
- An emotion that you found challenging
- A plan of action for something
- Recording things that make you happy
- Recording things that make you worry
- Things you can do to make things better or cheer yourself up

- Note down your values
- Work through any beliefs that you're not sure about
- Make big decisions using the making decisions exercise below

You can also use your journal to work through any problems as they come up. Try the useful Problem Solving exercise to help you do just that.

WHY IS USING A JOURNAL A GOOD IDEA?

Writing a journal helps you to check in with yourself, with your thoughts and emotions and the behaviours you're displaying as a result of them. You could say that your journal is like a personal record of your well-being.

It will help you get to know yourself better, build your self-esteem and resilience, and give you all the knowledge you need to know about yourself to make any necessary changes. Your self-awareness will rocket, and you'll be able to see your progress the more you use your journal to work through any difficulties as they show up.

Getting everything out of your head and down on paper is a great way of downloading your day and clearing your mind. You don't just have to write in it; you can doodle your thoughts or feelings on the page. Some days can feel like your head is on the fast spin of a washing machine, so getting it all out onto paper where you can start to make sense of it all is incredibly helpful. Making lists of things you need to remember, and things you need to do is another good way of relieving the stress of trying to keep everything spinning in your head.

PROBLEM-SOLVING EXERCISE

What is the problem you need to solve?

1. What are the possible solutions to the problem? Write down as many as you can think of

2. Pick three of the solutions you wrote down

3. What would be two advantages and disadvantages of choosing each of your three solutions?

4. Pick the best solution out of the three based on weighing the advantages and disadvantages

5. Decide when you're going to take action on the solution you have chosen and then do it

6. What was the outcome?

   Did your chosen solution work? If yes, that's great. What did you learn from doing this exercise, and what can you do in similar situations knowing what you now know? If not, don't worry. Sometimes it can take two or three attempts to find the right solution. Remind yourself of the other solutions you wrote down. Choose one of those and repeat the process.

TALK IT OUT

We girls are well known for enjoying a chat. We're generally better at talking things out than boys. We like to get together with friends and ask for advice, so if you have a trusted adult or a friend who you can talk to (and I mean really talk to) about your bad days and good ones, then you are lucky. Not everyone has that.

Be mindful about who you're talking to and whether they're the right person(s). It would help if you had someone who would listen from an outside perspective, has no invested interest in the outcome and would create a space for you to make your own decision. Your friends will want to help, which is great, but they can often tell you what they think you want to hear rather than give advice based on your current situation. They may want to influence your decision based on their agenda. They may want to control your decision to suit them. They may make things worse by creating an emotional frenzy where you get more emotionally charged about your current situation rather than encouraging you to seek reality to re-balance your emotional and rational mind.

Talking things out can help you to see things from a different perspective which means you can step outside of your thoughts and feelings and see things from the other person's point of view. You can use the Perspective exercise in Chapter 7 to help with this

I'm sure you know someone who is 'that friend.' The one who will challenge your thinking and tell you the truth, even if it stings at that moment. You know they have your best interests at heart, won't take any nonsense and will question your motives. Hang onto that friend as they are the type who will genuinely support you and help you to re-balance your emotional and rational mind. They will help you find the reality, and you'll want them in your corner.

If you can't think of a friend like that, then maybe YOU are that friend!

I AM that friend, and it's one of the reasons I now do what I do, as it's always been natural for me to see all angles of a situation, challenge thinking patterns and ask those questions that others are too scared to ask.

I've said this before, but it's so important that I will repeat it. If you're finding that your thoughts are getting the better of you and affecting your daily life, please let a trusted adult know who can help you find the right support. Counselling and Cognitive Behavioural Therapy are two great talking therapies that can support you in this.

CHAPTER TWELVE

SOCIAL MEDIA

I couldn't write this book and not talk about social media!

The world of technology is one that, as a teenager, allows you to be in 24-hour contact with the outside world, which is amazing. When my generation was teenagers, we had one phone in the house, attached to the wall in the living room where everyone could hear our conversation with our friends, and we were only allowed to make calls at certain times of the day when the call rate was cheaper.

A computer was a massive clunky thing that had to fire up for about five minutes before you could use it, and all you had was a black screen where you could write, and we had NO INTERNET. Can you even begin to imagine a world without the internet? Honestly, even my generation would now be lost without the internet, satnav, mobiles and Uber.

We now live in a world where you can purchase anything over the internet or your phone without getting out of bed. It sounds like bliss, doesn't it, and yes, at times, it's a great thing to have. But there are times when all this constant sensory stimulation can overwhelm you and affect your mental health as your brain isn't allowed to switch off.

Then we've got this whole world of social media that allows us to be nosy into the lives of millions of people. It's a world where some people will let you see the good and the

bad, and then you've got people who will only show you the best bits they have carefully curated for the world to see. The not 'perfect' parts will be left out, which is so fake. No one's life is always good; no one lives a life of posed photos on the beach and curated decor, fine dining and flawless skin and bodies, and unfortunately, Instagram is the worst place for all this fakeness. Yet, it's one of the places teenagers hang out the most, alongside TikTok and Snapchat.

The instant gratification you get from a like, comment or share on social media stimulates your brain and releases Dopamine. This pleasure chemical then rewards your brain, so your brain instantly wants more of that, and you get caught in the trap of the scroll or the need for more instant gratification. As this need grows, your neural pathways rewire in your brain, making it more challenging for you to stop scrolling. Five minutes turns into half an hour which turns into an hour, and so on. Before you know it, your mind is in overload, your need for instant pleasure is on high alert, and you can no longer think clearly, which is why when someone tries to talk to you whilst you're in this state, you don't hear them, see them, or understand what they're saying. You become completely disconnected from the world around you.

SOCIAL MEDIA AND BODY IMAGE

As a result, I have witnessed young girls comparing themselves to these fake stories, images and lives and wanting to completely change their appearance to match up to this so-called 'perfect - living my best life' brand that has become so popular.

This is causing a rise in young girls struggling with their body image because they feel like they're not skinny, tall, pretty, or tanned enough. Their lips aren't big enough, their eyebrows aren't tidy enough, and their self-esteem plummets are a result.

Yes, before the likes of Instagram, we still had some of this. However, the 24/7 barrage of images means that as a teenager, it's more difficult to get away from unless you train the algorithm to show you something different, more balanced and more REAL. Or not use it at all or check in sparingly.

Instagram is a great platforms for ideas, inspiration, and business, but it can also be a place that can make you feel bad about yourself, so choose who you follow wisely, curate a real life and attract others who are real too.

My girls and I follow an ex-model on Instagram who is amazing. She creates videos where she shows you how influencers and models pose to make their bodies look the way they do in photos and next to that, she shows you how she looks in everyday life, and the two are incredibly different. She talks about body confidence and how even having cellulite as a young girl is normal; bloating is inevitable after eating, at that time of the month or after having too much sugar etc. I encouraged my girls to follow her when they both started to pay more attention to their bodies, and we talked about some of her content when we were all together.

If you're finding that you're comparing yourself to a lot of these influencers, unfollow them. Choose to follow people who

are letting you see the authentic version of themselves - the ones who let you into the not-so-pretty side of what they do.

The same goes for TikTok. You can have a lot of fun on this platform. Through Covid, it was a great place to create videos, show off your dancing (or embarrass yourself in my case), or be inspired to create new hairstyles, makeup tutorials and creative tips and tricks. Still, it has its dark side where people try to encourage others to do things they wouldn't normally do, to be someone they're not and try risky or even dangerous things.

Social media platforms are primarily full of fake news and information. It's forever bombarding you with hearsay or gossip and can lead to confusion as you're not sure what's true and what isn't.

The things I want to warn young girls about the most when it comes to social media and phones are:

- Don't send pictures of yourself to people that are private or that you don't want to get out into the wider world.
- Don't send a picture of other people that you have no permission to share.
- Keep your social media accounts private.
- Block anyone who appears less than genuine or sends messages without your permission.
- Don't let other people log into your SM accounts, even if it's a friend.
- Password protect your phone.
- Turn off notifications so that you're not constantly being pinged and binged.

- Put a do not disturb on your phone at certain times of the day to take some time away from the noise.
- Put your phone down, walk away from it and do something else for a few hours. It's not going anywhere, and neither is the world within it, but if you don't look up once in a while, the real world will pass you by.

If you find it hard to put down your phone and leave it, turn it off for a while. Do this in 5-10 minutes stages until you get up to at least an hour or two. I know you're thinking, 'what on earth is she saying? There's no way I can do that.' Let me assure you that you can and will thank me for it in the long term, I promise.

Social media is to you what TV was to my generation.

When I was a kid, we had the TV. These days it's not the big box in the corner of the room but the small device that is constantly in your hand. Our parents hated us sitting staring at the TV all day, especially during the school holidays, so they would switch it off and tell us to go and do something else, go outside, read, or listen to music.

You want a healthy, balanced relationship with your phone and social media. If you need to distract yourself at first, go to the 'Ways to Improve Your Well-being' chapter and get some ideas on what you could be doing and how you can relax your mind. Taking a break from technology as a whole will positively affect your physical and emotional well-being.

Let me assure you, though, that it is not just you teenagers

who can benefit from this chapter. I'm sure you will have noticed that, as a society, we have become fixated on our phones. We use them for absolutely everything, which is great news for the technology companies but not so much good news for our health and well-being.

The overall need for Dopamine has overtaken the need for connection, which is a worrying effect. I see families all staring at their phones instead of connecting, and then they wonder why they have nothing to say, why they aren't getting on and why they feel like they don't know each other anymore. As humans, we are made for connection and community, yet here we all are taking instant pleasure over a connection, community and long-term happiness. Pleasure is short-term, so we start to crave more, which feeds addiction, whereas connection and happiness are long-term rewards which we can grow in a healthy and balanced way.

My Nan always said, "everything in moderation," which is worth remembering for everything in life. Balance your phone time with non-phone time, and you won't go far wrong.

Pleasure is about taking and comes from things we rely on outside of ourselves. Happiness is about giving and experiences that we feel from within. Remember pleasure is short-term, and happiness and health are long-term.

CHAPTER THIRTEEN

INNER CONFIDENCE

At least half of all adolescents struggle with low confidence during their early teenage years.

As a teenager, you're faced with several challenging issues present during this time. Challenges such as the physical and emotional changes you go through, topped with changes in hormone levels, school transitions, friendships, romantic relationships and interests and learning how to deal with them can take a toll on your confidence levels.

I was working with a young girl not so long ago who told me that she lacked the confidence to be like all the other girls. I asked her what the other girls were like, and she said they were more confident. When I asked her why she thought this, she said they were louder than her, wore better clothes, had more friends and wore their make-up better. I asked her why she considered those things to mean they were more confident than she, and she replied that she had been told when she was younger that that's what confident girls looked and sounded like.

When she was younger, an older cousin told her that if she wanted to be in with the confident girls at school, she had to dress and act a certain way. This had stuck with her, and as a result, she believed that if you weren't any of the things her cousin had mentioned, then you weren't confident.

We worked through this belief, and I asked her what confidence meant to her. We discovered that being louder and dressing differently wasn't what it was all about. For her, it was about being comfortable in her own skin, being able to do the things she wanted and not worrying about what others thought. She wanted others to accept her for being more reserved, less glamorous and a deep thinker.

We talked through whether she genuinely thought that the louder girls who wore the same clothes and make-up as all the others were really all that confident within themselves. Or were they doubting themselves and lacking the confidence to be their authentic selves by blending in with everyone else. She'd never really thought about it that way, but realising that they too might be lacking confidence in one area or another made her feel better about herself.

Take a few minutes to think about what confidence means to you, what areas you believe you have confidence in, and what areas you feel you need to work on to gain confidence.

Being louder can often be mistaken for confidence when it actually might be masking that all too well-known insecurity of not feeling good enough. You can be quieter and have great inner confidence.

You may spend much time worrying about what people think of you. When the truth is, people spend more time worrying about what others think about them than worrying about you! You see, inner confidence comes from self-acceptance and from realising that other people have their insecurities and are more worried about their flaws than they ever are about yours.

CIRCLE OF CONFIDENCE EXERCISE

You can use your imagination to bring about confidence, self-belief and calm. Use this technique in many ways; to build confidence, relieve anxiety and boost self-belief. It's worth learning this so you can use it as a resource in many situations. You can ask a trusted adult to do this with you the first time if you're not too sure. They will benefit from it too.

1. Identify the situation that you want to go well or improve, e.g. reading aloud at school, playing sports, meeting new people, or going to new places. Decide how you want to feel in this situation, e.g. more confident, more motivated or calmer.
2. Set up, either in your mind or physically, using a piece of paper or even a hula hoop, a 'circle of confidence.' Notice what colour it is and how big it is. Make sure it's big enough for you to be able to step into.
3. Think back to the feeling you wanted to have about your chosen situation. Once you feel the confidence, calm or motivation, either see yourself stepping into the circle in your mind or physically step into your circle on the floor. Keep that feeling with you as you do this and stay there for a minute or two.
4. Step back out of the circle and think of something completely different, e.g. what you're having for tea.
5. Step back into the circle, and that feeling of confidence, motivation or calm will return.
6. Think about an upcoming situation that would normally worry you and notice how it now feels different and less daunting.

Your confidence is related to your self-esteem, but having high self-esteem doesn't mean you always feel confident. Confidence can change throughout your life and is affected by significant life changes, like transitioning into secondary school, college or work.

When confidence drops, it can lead to bad decisions, riskier behaviours and unhealthy relationships. You are better equipped to make better decisions and build healthier relationships by boosting your confidence levels.

Here are some signs of **self-confidence** in young people:

- A generally good posture
- Bright and alert eyes with good levels of eye contact
- A relaxed walk and general demeanour
- Can give and accept praise
- Open to feedback from others
- Has a curious nature around new ideas
- Able to cope with change easily

Here are some signs of **low self-confidence** in young people:

- Unable to accept praise
- Speaking negatively about themselves
- Walking with their head down and hair covering their face
- Unable to make eye contact
- Often talk negatively about other people
- Hold back in class or social situations
- Easily influenced by peers
- Think they will fail at whatever they try and do or refuse to try new things

When you're not feeling your confident self, your Inner Critic, the one who wants to keep you safe but also stuck, can take over your mind and cause a lot of inner chatter that isn't true. One way to move your Inner Critic aside is to introduce your Inner Coach. She is your cheerleader and the positive, confident self who is here to fight back and put your inner critic back in its place.

Remaining firmly in your comfort zone can signify that your confident self has taken a break. You will have been more willing to try new things as a young child. Let's face it, if you hadn't, learning to walk, talk, eat and ride your bike would have been impossible. You were able to go to new places and do scary things like meet new people and join a playgroup where you didn't know anyone. But in your teenage years, the fear of the unknown, embarrassment and judgement have kicked in, and you're sticking firmly in the safe and warm space of your comfort zone at all times.

As much as your comfort zone feels safe, warm and familiar to you, it's also restricting your growth. Stepping outside of it may feel scary, but on the other side of that fear are new and exciting experiences, and your new bigger comfort zone is waiting with open arms to make you feel welcome. Try the Overcoming the Fear Excercise to learn new techniques for overcoming the fear.

You can also create an anchor to help you tap into the feeling of confidence when you need to. You can find out how in the 'Ways to Improve Your Well-being chapter. Or use the circle of confidence.

USE YOUR INNER COACH EXERCISE

This is how you can use your Inner Coach effectively:

1. Imagine that your Inner Critic is a person.
2. Give them a name.
3. What do they look like?
4. What do they sound like?
5. What are they wearing?
6. Now imagine that they are sitting opposite you.
7. Imagine your Inner Coach is a person.
8. Give them a name.
9. What do they look like?
10. What do they sound like?
11. What are they wearing?
12. Step into your Inner Coach and be them.
13. What do you (your Inner Coach) want to say to your Inner Critic?

14. Ask your Inner Critic what they want.

15. Thank Inner Critic for coming and keeping you safe and within your comfort zone, but tell them that you've got things from here and that they can leave now.

16. Notice how you feel having sent your Inner Critic on their way.

You can repeat this exercise whenever you need to.

OVERCOMING THE FEAR EXCERCISE

A few things you can do to overcome the fear:

- Make a list of the worst outcomes and rank them from 1 (not at all likely) to 10 (very likely) in order of how likely they are to happen.
- List the times you have taken a risk and stepped out of your comfort zone.
- Write down what you learned from each of those previous experiences.
- Do the Inner Critic vs Inner Coach exercise and tell yourself, "I've got this!"
- Take a step back as if leaving your body and view what's happening from an outside perspective.
- What do you see?
- What do you want to say to yourself?

I first heard the saying "confidence is in the doing" when I was doing my Neuro Linguistic Programming Practitioner training, and it stuck with me because it's so very true. When you're first learning how to do something, you're not yet confident in your ability to do it well, but you have to do it to get better at it and succeed. Yet most people don't even want to try it until they know they will be good at it. You can see where the issue lies in this one, can't you?

Using the above tools, you can start 'doing' and building your inner confidence and support those around you to do the same.

CHAPTER FOURTEEN

SELF-HARM AS A RESULT OF BULLYING & BODY SHAMING

I can't write a book for young girls without including support regarding bullying, body image and self-harm. More and more young girls are turning to self-harm as a coping strategy, and that's a pretty scary thought for any parent or caregiver. The reasons are unclear, but there is so much pressure to be a certain way to be accepted. The fact that as young girls, you're exposed to more and more images online of what society considers a perfect life, a perfect body, the perfect relationship, being the perfect student, and getting the perfect grades, it's no wonder that the stress of feeling you have to meet all of these unrealistic and quite frankly dangerous expectations is too much for some girls to deal with.

I also believe that young girls are turning to social media platforms to talk about self-harm and the relief it gives them and that other girls are giving it a try because they believe that these girls are trying to help. But I need you to be very careful here as it appears to be becoming a trend for people to glamorise self-harm where they're actively encouraging young people to carry out explicit acts of harm to themselves. If you think you've been exposed to this kind of behaviour, please tell a trusted adult as this is incredibly dangerous and wrong for people to be enticing vulnerable people to hurt themselves.

I'm here to give you some advice and help you to understand the dangers of using self-harm as a coping strategy. I'm speaking as a parent, a practitioner, and from my own teen years (I chose some risky behaviours due to peer pressure and things that happened during this time). I struggled with things linked to my body image, my first boyfriend and how I felt I didn't fit in.

For a moment, though, let's think about the reasons why a young girl may choose to self-harm. I'm going to use my own teenage experience here.

I mentioned earlier in this book that I was a gymnast as a child and up until the age of seventeen, when like many young people, I wanted my life back. I wanted more freedom to go out, be with my friends and earn some money. During my gymnast days, the head coach of one particular gymnasium outwardly bullied me in front of the other girls and made sure that I knew without any doubt that he didn't think I should be there. This took a toll on my confidence and self-esteem. It went on for some time, and I got used to it after a while. I got on with it and started to believe that I didn't deserve to be there and that I was no good. This was the beginning of me not feeling 'good enough', and this belief became deeply buried in my mind. After that, I was always looking to back up this thought in all areas of my life; in my first romantic relationship, friendship group, how I looked and dressed and when I started work. You name it, and I looked for the evidence to back up the belief I had taken on when I was ten.

As a petite girl, both in height and weight, I had grown

used to being called too small, too short, too skinny. Most people believe that if you're small and slim, you're protected from body image shaming, but that's not the case, and I have worked with many young girls who have felt body shamed for having too skinny legs and too skinny wrists. They hide their bodies underneath black clothing just as much as those who are self-conscious due to being too tall, too big, too pale etc. Any type of body shaming affects young people, so if you've been guilty of commenting on a friend's appearance, please think about the impact this might have on them.

Your self-talk will also have a big impact on your body image, so please speak kinder to yourself and have compassion for how amazing your body is and what it does for you each day. Give yourself daily compliments on a different part of your body and compliment your friends too. Build each other up and help to support each other's body image. If you hear a friend talking negatively about themselves, ask them to name three parts of their body that they like and three parts of their body that have helped them in some way that day. Do the same thing for yourself too. This switches your focus and stops that negative thinking spiral from growing, freeing you from the spirals power.

Remember that every girl you meet struggles to accept at least one or two parts of her body right now, so be kind to them and yourself.

I was exposed to this form of bullying again in secondary school and became so self-conscious of how I looked that I hid my body under baggy clothes. As I got older, my body began to change, and I started to form more curves around

my hips, which is very natural and part of becoming a woman. I began to worry that I would no longer have the flat tum-my that everyone commented on and that I would no longer be skinny. I started to obsess about being everything everyone had told me I was up until this point. My inner critic began to speak very loudly to me, saying that I needed to stay small, skinny and all the things that I now believed to be true about me. Changing and being told anything else scared me. I didn't want to go through any other kind of name calling or change that would impact how I saw myself. The pressure of becoming known as anything different got too much. As a result, I started to take laxatives regularly, hoping to stop myself from putting on any weight and ensure I had a flat tummy at all times. This was not possible and completely unrealistic, but I had to stay the same.

This went on for years until I was in my early 30s. I didn't feel good enough unless I was at my smallest. I would eat chocolate, crisps, and all the things you're told are not good for you, and then I would go home and take laxatives that night to get rid of it all. But here's the thing; laxatives don't actually work like that; it is dangerous to use them this way, but I wasn't interested in the dangers. All I cared about was being 'good enough' for other people! I would even plan the nights I would take them around whatever plans I had that week. If I felt like my tummy was bloated for whatever reason, which is perfectly natural, having eaten, I would convince myself that I needed to take some that night.

There were nights when I would be up in the middle of the night. On occasion, I would pass out and have a fit due to having taken too many or taken them too frequently for my body to handle, but it didn't stop me at the time. I must mention that laxative abuse seriously affects your body's ability to do its job correctly. It can lead to permanent damage to the digestive system. It can cause severe dehydration leading to body tremors, long-term kidney damage, and a complete loss of control of the colon.

As the years passed, I started to forget why I even started taking them in the first place, but I kept going. It had become a habit I couldn't break; it had taken hold of me and controlled my life. Eventually, having had one fit too many in a short time, I realised that I was hurting myself and making myself ill for something that no one was even worried about anymore. The only person still holding onto the idea that I had to be a certain way was me. Everyone else had moved on. I didn't see many of these people anymore, yet here they were, affecting my day-to-day life and controlling how I lived.

Back then, if you had told me that what I was doing was a form of self-harm, I would never have believed you because no one ever talked about self-harm in those days. When I discovered that self-harm was so much more than scratching and cutting yourself, the penny dropped, and I recognised that I had been causing my body harm to control a situation that I couldn't control, and it had taken control of me.

Shame is one of the strongest emotions behind self-harm, and I, for one, felt a huge amount of it, which is why I never told anyone about my laxative abuse. I kept it a secret because of the guilt of what I was doing. I knew it was wrong and harmful, and the guilt grew stronger the longer I continued until it became shame. You see, guilt and shame

are very closely linked. Guilt is when you know you've made a mistake and feel bad about what you did. Shame is about feeling bad about who you are. So if you continue to feel guilty about what you're doing, you will start feeling bad about who you're becoming, which can cause more harm as you dislike yourself further.

Like many young people when it comes to coping with life's stressors, I felt isolated and carried around a lot of that shame due to the secret. One of my values has always been honesty, so keeping this from the people I loved felt wrong, but it wasn't something I wanted to worry them with. They had their own worries to deal with; why would they want to worry about mine too? Being a burden was something I never wanted to be, but when I look back, I could have saved myself years of lying to myself and the people I love. I could have gotten the support I needed to find a better way to cope, which also would have re-leased those feelings of shame. Shame has no power over you when you release its grasp, and to see that the solution of taking the laxatives in the first place was now the problem would have helped me to overcome it and find the reality in the situation so I could have moved on.

Talking is one of the most powerful ways to take shame's power away, so please find a trusted adult to confide in, or even call the Samaritans or text YoungMinds (you can find details on the resources page).

Drinking, smoking, taking drugs, scratching, cutting - anything that is abusing your body, either inside or outside, due to a need to control emotions, situations or thoughts or to 'FEEL' something due to the numbness felt inside, can be considered self-harm. Knowing this really hit me as I got older and is a crucial factor in why I wrote this book. I don't want any young girl to feel like she needs to turn to such coping strategies and feel like they're alone or not good enough. YOU are good enough, NO MATTER WHAT!

Now, going out for a few drinks and having one too many occasionally is normal (I'm talking about when it's legal, of course); trying out smoking is also very normal and both are behaviours that young people experiment with, even drugs. It's all part of those riskier behaviours young people partake in due to the emotional brain still being very much in control. However, I don't recommend or condone any of these bad habits.

When it becomes a problem, it starts to dictate, take over and control your day-to-day life. It also becomes a problem for those around you. You begin to become isolated as a result or your behaviour towards yourself and others changes, and you start to cover up and lie about how much, how often, and the impact of what you're doing negatively affects you and others.

The NICE guidelines define self-harm as: "self-poisoning or injury, irrespective of the apparent purpose of the act".

If any part of my story resonates with you or someone you love, please get in touch with a trusted adult for help. If you don't feel you can do this within your immediate circle, you can always turn to YoungMinds; a charity set up, especially for young people. You can use their text service for support **(www.youngminds.org.uk)** or mind **(www.mind.org.uk)**. Both these are good places to start seeking help.

Controlled eating, sending risky images of yourself, and putting yourself in dangerous situations can all be self-harming behaviours. Would you believe me if I told you that seeking out fights was a form of self-harm? I know I wouldn't have when I was young, but think about it. If you're seeking to physically harm another person knowing that you're going to get hurt yourself, and you're purposefully putting yourself in harm's way, then you are looking to be hurt. Why are you looking to be hurt? Because you feel or think that you need to feel that hurt. Now, there are many different reasons why you may feel this need. You may have felt numb due to a situation or circumstance, so feeling something, even if it's a pain, is better than feeling nothing. This is also how people who scratch or cut themselves can feel, too, and this is something that a professional can support you to overcome. They will work with you to find other strategies to better support you and overcome the need in time.

When you choose to harm yourself in any way, the relief from the pressure or the stress is only short-term, so the need for the relief grows over time, just like it did for me when I was using laxatives. The truth is these short-term solutions actually become the problem. Like for me, I forgot the original problem, and those people had moved on, yet I was stuck in the short-term solution that became the problem.

Thanks to the Human Givens 'How to Reduce and Overcome Self-harm' course that I took, I can bring you this beneficial resource to help you if you feel that you may be using or are tempted to start using any form of self-harming behaviours.

THE SELF-MANAGEMENT PLAN

1. What are the triggers for my self-harm/when do I most feel like doing it?

2. How do I know that I'm starting to feel bad? What are your mind and body telling you at this point?

3. What are the physical signs?

4. What's the emotion you're feeling?

5. What are you thinking?

6. What behaviours are you displaying as a result?

STOP

1. Discover some immediate ways to cope and reduce the initial adrenaline levels.

2. Phone a close friend

3. Take a walk, even if it's just around your garden

4. Using a breathing technique - see 7-11 breathing in chapter 10

5. Play your favourite music and sing at the top of your lungs

1. Use the grounding technique from the improving your well-being chapter

2. Count backwards from 100

CALM DOWN

6. Write down the thoughts you're having and put them on trial. See chapter 8

7. Swap your favourite loud music and switch to something relaxing. It could be music, running water, nature, or birds singing.

8. Go out for a longer walk, in nature if possible.

9. Clean something - such as your room. It's incredibly therapeutic in these situations.

10. The aim here is to focus outside yourself first to distract the mind and then bring you back into balance and re-regulate your thoughts and emotions. Repeat when necessary.

Looking back at your Emotional Needs in chapter 10 will support you to re-balance yourself and even potentially figure out, with the help of a loved one or professional, how you can healthily meet those needs in balance moving forward.

I've already said it a few times in this chapter, but please seek help if any of this sounds familiar to you. I promise you that opening up about your struggles will enable you to start the road to healing, and the sooner that starts, the sooner you can feel free from the pressures of self-harm.

CHAPTER FIFTEEN

REASONS TO STAY IN BED

I want to thank you for coming on this journey with me and for sticking with it. As a young person, it can feel challenging to see things like this through, so give yourself a big pat on the back and be very proud of yourself.

When you go in and do the work to create more confidence and self-esteem and discover self-acceptance, you can feel lonely. Having read this book, though, you may feel like isolating yourself further due to learning more about yourself, and I see this a lot. Many people around you won't understand your journey, and that's okay. They don't have to understand. You just need them to support you through it, and one way you can do that is to introduce them to this book for themselves. It is up to them if they choose to read it, but it will help them understand why you're changing your own path.

I call this stage of the process the chrysalis phase. You see, as a young child, you're the caterpillar, and you want to be the butterfly in your adult years. But the caterpillar has to go in on himself into the chrysalis to create the necessary changes to emerge as the vibrant butterfly. A creature that can fly, is bright in colour and is proud to be able to do the things he couldn't do as a caterpillar. He flies with confidence and acceptance that he has changed. It's quite a transformation, and he does it alone, and as humans, sometimes we have to do the same.

The caterpillar cannot talk, but as a human, you can, so although you may travel this journey mostly alone, remember that there are people out there who want to help. Keep this in mind as you grow, and it will help you through this transformation. If you don't feel like you can turn to a family member, friend, teacher, tutor etc., then there is a list of places ready and waiting to support you on the resources page at the end.

At this point, it's common for your fight, flight or freeze mode to kick in. You've just learned a lot about how you can become the version of yourself that you want to be, and the techniques you can use in pretty much any situation can feel overwhelming. The details in this book may be swimming around in your head whilst you have no idea where to start. It's a lot, I know, but I want you to know that it's perfectly natural and completely okay. But I don't want you to walk away from this book having not implemented any of the life-changing techniques and advice you have spent time reading and absorbing. After reading this book until this point, you must have recognised that you wanted to create some change.

I know there will be at least 3-5 techniques that you read that you thought were helpful, so if you're unsure where to start, start with those. Chat to your family about your and their needs. It's a great place to start and where I start with all the teenagers and families I work with.

One of the lines I hear from nearly every teenager I work with is..."but it's just loooooong!"

Picture me slumped over my desk as I type this with a long face with little or no energy, as this is how I see many of the young people I work with when they're faced with something they find challenging or if they don't know where to start.

Don't worry; I've got you. This book isn't just for one read; it's for you to refer back to, so turn the corners of the most valuable pages to highlight them. And then, when you need to, you can turn to that chapter and re-read the relevant section. So if you feel like this is looooooong, come back to it when you recognise that something is happening that you're not too sure of how to handle. You can also keep this as a guide and hand it down to your kids one day.

If I've learnt anything about young people, and indeed myself, it's that when we go to school and face exams and tests, we start to believe that we have to keep everything in our heads and if we don't, we're failing. This is just nonsense. No one is expecting you to re-member everything you've read here either and be able to put the book aside and know everything just like that. No one can carry that information around with them all the time.

One of the reasons for this book is for you to have something you can always turn to for support. Most people I work with carry my voice in their minds and ask themselves, "What would Faye say to me now?" "What would Faye do here?" You can't do that as you can't hear my voice, but you can similarly reference my words.

You can take this journey one step at a time, and I am

right here with you, on your book-shelf, in your bag, but please don't put me in the back of your drawer. I get a little claustrophobic in small spaces.

CHAPTER SIXTEEN

ACTION TAKING MAKING THE DIFFERENCE

Now is the time to start taking action. You've done the hardest part by picking up this book and reading it to the end, giving yourself permission to gain the information and tools needed to implement those changes.

You can gather all the information, knowledge and tools, but if you don't take action on any of it, you will stay in the same place. For now, that might feel okay, but as time goes by, you're going to want to take action, and taking one small action now will set you on the path you want to take. One small step leads to another until one day you look back and see that those small actions have all added to the bigger one of where you wanted to go. Your action steps have given you the confidence to go after what you want and be the person you want to be.

Use this book as your guide to making sense of yourself and the world around you, and you won't go far wrong.

And if at any point you'd like more support with anything I've included within these pages, you can find me at www.fayecoxcoaching.co.uk where you will find further information and support, including details about the increasingly popular 'Needs Audit.'

CHAPTER SEVENTEEN

YOUR CHOICE

Throughout this book, I have been giving you a clear message that I want you to take through the rest of your life. YOU ARE GOOD ENOUGH, NO MATTER WHAT!

I can't stress this enough. The feeling of not being good enough is the underlying emotion that stops many people from taking the action they need to create the life they want. It holds back so many of the young people I work with, and here you are, having read the book, in a great place to start taking that action and creating the life you deserve.

This book has enabled you to let go of shame, guilt, and limiting beliefs and set you on the road to self-compassion, self-trust, and, most importantly, self-acceptance.

I know this is possible for you. How? Because I've seen it, I've participated and done it my-self.

I have witnessed and been a part of some incredible young people's journeys from self-doubt, shame, anger and inner conflict to inner confidence, self-belief and self-acceptance. Each story I've told in this book is relevant to a young person who has changed things within their life that they didn't think or feel possible before.

My favourite of all these stories was the lad who believed that he only deserved to be 'bad,' that, that was the way it was for him and he couldn't be anything else. People had repeatedly told him that he was no good, would never amount to anything, and was on the road to nowhere! Then we sat down and chatted about where that came from and where he wanted to go in life. Not where he reckoned he would end up, but where did he want life to take him? What did he want life to look like? It was then that he realised that he had a choice. Yes, he could decide what the future held for him, not all the people who had told him otherwise. He saw in his mind that he could take a different path, and as a result, he started making the changes needed to get himself where he wanted to go. He's still a work in progress, the same as the rest of us. But now, he has a plan, direction, a purpose and the be-lief that he is good enough.

Finally, I'd like to leave you with this:

"You get to choose who you want to be"

CONNECT WITH ME

Website

- www.fayecoxcoaching.co.uk

Email

- faye@fayecoxcoaching.co.uk

Purchase these resources on my website

I am enough journal
Affirmation and gratitude journal
Confidence boost journal
Family well-being toolkit
Self-Love Affirmation cards

- www.fayecoxcoaching.co.uk/shop

USEFUL LINKS

MENTAL HEALTH CHARITIES

YoungMinds - **www.youngminds.org.uk/**
or text **YM** to **85258**
Mind - **www.mind.org.uk**
CAMHS - **www.nhs.uk/nhs-services/mental-health-services/mental-health-services-for-young-people/children-young-people-mental-health-services-cypmhs/**
Harmless - **www.harmless.org.uk**
The Samaritans - **Call 116 123** or text **SHOUT** to **85258**

DETAILS OF THE PRACTICES I USED WITHIN THIS BOOK

Human Givens - **www.humangivens.com**
NLP - **www.medicalnewstoday.com/articles/320368**
CBT - **www.nhs.uk/mental-health/talking-therapies-medicine-treatments/talking-therapies-and-counselling/cognitive-behavioural-therapy-cbt/overview/**

MEDITATION APPS TO HELP YOU GET STARTED

You-Tube - **www.youtube.com** search for meditation for young people
Calm - **www.calm.com**
Headspace - **www.headspace.com**

THINGS I WANT YOU TO ALWAYS REMEMBER

- You're not for everyone, and that's okay.
- Your academic achievements do not determine your self-worth.
- Learn to ride the wave of your emotions.
- Confidence is in the doing.
- Fitting in is becoming who you think you need to be in order to be accepted. Belonging is being your authentic self and knowing that no matter what happens, you belong to you. (Brene Brown)
- Failure and rejection are redirections.
- You can't control anything except how you choose to respond.
- You are allowed to say NO.
- You don't have to have all the answers now.

THINGS I WANT YOU TO ALWAYS REMEMBER CONTINUED

- Practice the PAUSE before judging, assuming, accusing and whenever you're about to react to something, and you'll be able to avoid doing and saying things that you may regret later.
- Hurt people, hurt people.
- You don't have to attend every argument that you're invited to.
- You can allow others to be wrong without the need to tell them so.
- Learn to respond rather than react.
- Other people's behaviour is about THEM. Your behaviour is about YOU.
- Remember to BREATHE!
- YOU ARE GOOD ENOUGH, NO MATTER WHAT!